THE FALCONS OF DESIRE

GUERNICA WORLD EDITIONS 87

Frank Lentricchia

THE FALCONS OF DESIRE

TORONTO—CHICAGO—BUFFALO—LANCASTER (U.K.)

2024

Guernica Editions Founder: Antonio D'Alfonso

Michael Mirolla, editor
Cover and interior design: Errol F. Richardson

Guernica Editions Inc.
1241 Marble Rock Rd., Gananoque (ON), Canada K7G 2V4
2250 Military Road, Tonawanda, N.Y. 14150-6000 U.S.A.
www.guernicaeditions.com

Distributors:
Independent Publishers Group (IPG)
600 North Pulaski Road, Chicago IL 60624
University of Toronto Press Distribution (UTP)
5201 Dufferin Street, Toronto (ON), Canada M3H 5T8

First edition.
Printed in Canada.

Legal Deposit—Third Quarter
Library of Congress Catalog Card Number: 2024930549
Library and Archives Canada Cataloguing in Publication
Title: The falcons of desire / Frank Lentricchia.
Names: Lentricchia, Frank, author.
Series: Guernica world editions (Series) ; 87.
Description: First edition. | Series statement: Guernica world editions ; 87
Identifiers: Canadiana (print) 20240288211 | Canadiana (ebook) 2024028822X | ISBN
9781771839310 (softcover) | ISBN 9781771839327 (EPUB)
Subjects: LCGFT: Novels.
Classification: LCC PS3562.E57 F35 2024 | DDC 813/.54—dc23

For Lou Renza

Natives of poverty, children of malheur,
The gaiety of language is our seigneur.
　　　　　　—**Wallace Stevens**, *Esthétique Du Mal*

THE RECEPTIONIST

(IN OCTOBER OF THAT YEAR)

At Hotel Utica The Receptionist sees an old man in a leather jacket. He's small. A little hunched over. He introduces himself as Rocky. He says, "I need to talk to one of your guests. A relative of mine. Maria Silvestri." The Receptionist says, "Rocky, if that's your name, which I doubt, I'm not a pimp for deteriorating seniors and their so-called relatives. Nice jacket."

*

The Receptionist observes in cold October the well-known Utica face of Richard Romano. He's wearing a gray herringbone sport jacket, T-shirt, and jeans. He does not address her. Sits across from the elevator, expectantly. The elevator will not open to his desire. When he rises, thwarted, he crosses to The Receptionist and says, "Tell her, put a message in her mailbox and write, <u>It's the time and place for us – Richard R.</u>" "Tell who?" she says. "Maria Silvestri. Don't play dumb." She says, "God bless you afford that jacket." The Receptionist thinks, I knew his wife in high school. That power-house bitch, Connie O'Donnell, if she finds out what he's doing here she'll ream him a new one.

*

As a heavy downpour floods the sewer-clogged streets of Utica, New York, The Receptionist observes a stocky man in a long overcoat. (Is he exposed under there?) Black curly hair. He approaches, book in hand. He says, "May I read you a poem?" She stares. He reads to her:

> *But at my back I always hear*
> *Time's winged chariot hurrying near.*

He says, "What do you think of that?" She stares. He says, "This poem is called *To His Coy Mistress*. Look. Read. Marvelous, don't you agree?" He tells her that he teaches at the college. Tells her he wants to speak with Maria Silvestri. He says, "I don't have much time left on the life meter."

She points to the exit. This so-called professor is a pervert.

*

He enters. A Utican feared across all neighborhoods. It's Russell Martello, who says, "Tell so-called Maria Silvestri that I'll take her to The Falcon tomorrow. 7 A.M. Tell her on behalf of The Falcon. The Falcon, tell her."

Martello in jeans and a tight-fitting T-shirt. Muscles bulging – neck, chest, arms. In high school, she thinks, he was a pudgy joke. He's become fuckable. Those muscles in this weather must keep him warm – even without a shirt he could walk around in this weather. With those lickable muscles.

EARLIER THAT YEAR: SUMMER

1.

She Walks In Beauty

ONE HOUR BEFORE she boards Alitalia from Naples to JFK, the Italian Stranger calls her uncle's special friend in Utica – Don Joseph (The Falcon) Furillo.

"This thing is not for the phone," Don Joseph says. "Wake up and smell the coffee."

She says, "I do not drink coffee."

He says, "Don't wise off. Uncle Carlo give you my address?"

She says, "Yes."

The line goes dead.

*

On her first day in Utica, a late afternoon in sweltering mid-August, she hires a taxi to carry her from Hotel Utica to a large two-family house on upper Taylor Ave, a short stone's throw below the high point of The Parkway, where the wealthy and the near wealthy reside. Upper Taylor is part of what is called Corn Hill, in memory of nineteenth-century Utica. Neither East, nor West, nor South Utica, and far from North Utica: Just Corn Hill, a section of town without firm geographical location, where The Falcon, of East Utica origin, chose to live – rather than in one of the exposed grand mansions, a few yards away, on The Parkway, that he could have easily afforded. His wife on the second story, he on the first, because why should he have to climb the stairs?

The Falcon's deep backyard is enclosed with eight foot barbed wire fencing, the top section of which slants inward to the yard at a 45° angle, and is electrified to a dangerous level, as dead squirrels at the base of his fence frequently attest. He hates squirrels.

He greets her in sunglasses and leads her, bearing a bowl of cool water, to the backyard, where they sit beneath a grape arbor, heavy with the fragrance of Pinot Noir fruit. He sets the bowl of water on the picnic table and proceeds to pluck many grapes, dropping them gently, one by one, into the water. He places the bowl before her. He looks up again to the massive hanging clusters, as he inhales deeply and says, "This is how I degenerate. Wine is not committed on my property."

She says, "I do not drink wine."

He says, "Or coffee. You please me. How greatly we will see."

The fragrance blanketing The Falcon and his Italian visitor mixes three stages of grape: the ripe, the overly ripe, and the rotten. Sweetness and putrefaction. She puts the ripe, the overly ripe, and the putrefying, one by one, slowly, between her lips, sucking deep before swallowing them whole.

He says, "You don't faze me with your mouth."

She says, "My face. Try to find it. It is always above the – how do you say in English? – The tits?"

He says, "What are you trying to put across, the way you dress?"

He removes his sunglasses.

He says, "I have eyes."

She had appeared at The Falcon's door in a so-called Yankees' cap – black, white-lettered insignia, worn now world-wide by those, like the Italian Stranger, who do not know or care about baseball, much less the Yankees. New York City. They love the idea of New York City.

Here she is in a red midriff-baring halter top, snug white shorts to mid-thigh, black running shoes. No socks.

She says, "The face. The tits are not the face."

He says, "I refuse to laugh."

"Don Furillo," she says, "I wish to speak to Rocco DiCastro, the godfather of Richard Romano. Privately. Can you help? Don Furillo, find the face."

He says, "Uncle Carlo informed me about your grandmother Maria Silvestri and Giulio Romano, and your grievance with Giulio. In this profession of mine we do not intervene with the domestic problems of civilians. Our specialty – we kill each other. Amongst ourselves, for comedy, we say internal annihilation is the true meaning of *Cosa Nostra*."

She says, "Soon we can do something very special. Together. Yes?"

*

The taxi driver had taken her from the city center at Hotel Utica, talking all the while into his head-set-connected cell phone, speaking neither English nor Italian. The route he took carried her from the base of Taylor Ave, rising all the way to The Falcon's house. What she had seen she rarely saw in her native Naples: vast two-story houses. So many. Only the rich could afford such things in Italy. In America, she thought, all are rich without taste for beauty, living in disgraceful houses of peeling clapboards, sagging roofs and porches crying for a carpenter. The closer the taxi got to The Parkway, the better these houses were maintained and The Falcon's house was the most attractive of them all, like the house of Uncle Carlo, where Carlo, who is rarely seen, spends his days doing work not to be discussed. Her father said, He is a serious man, my daughter, very serious, who is fond of you. Very fond.

*

Two weeks later, after she and The Falcon had done many special things for each other, she left The Falcon's bed with The Falcon's directions for a stroll down into the heart of the East Side, to Café Romano – known to regulars as "Richie's sweetheart." She walked up several yards to The Parkway, turned east until she reached Mohawk. At Mohawk and The Parkway, she headed down, falling ever down to the heart, passing along the way a graveyard – grave stones as far as she could see. Finally, Bleecker and the Lower East side, where she saw it, across Bleecker. Café Romano.

Sitting at a table facing the window, three Café regulars. They see her. How could they not? Gene says, hand over heart, "Oh yeah. There she goes, Miss America." Bob says, "Jesus Christ, Gene! I'm a leg man." "Christ Almighty!" Remo says, "this is wrong. At my age, you kidding me? I play 36 holes at my age, but the only hole that – forget about it. If I had a fuckin' Rosary I'd ask the Virgin – Blessed Mother of God grant me one last favor and your Son can take me right after. Hail Mary, full of grace, the Lord is with thee so forth."

She does not enter the Café. She walks instead deeply east along Bleecker, looking for Bacon Street, where it crosses Bleecker, to turn right off Bleecker, and walk one block up to Mary Street.

Now, in twilight, at the corner of Bacon and Mary, she stops to gaze at Richie Romano's house, lips slightly parted. 1303 Mary.

*

They would come forward – men, exclusively – "witnesses," they called themselves, to her presence in North, South, West, and East Utica. Some said she was dropped off by taxi into the neighborhood and proceeded to walk on the same street twice, three times, often stopping for no discernible reason and staring. At what? Why does she walk? Stroll, not walk? Without destination? She's not walking or strolling. She's gliding. As if her feet don't touch the ground.

Someone said she was casing the neighborhood. Seeing who's home, who's not. Who's got a security system, who doesn't. I thought about calling the cops, but I didn't. I should've. Who was she working for? I could say, but I won't because I'm not crazy. Don't quote me. I'll deny everything, including saying she's totally hot. Which she was and I hope still is, God help her. Movie-star looks. So she's walking around the West Side where we Polish people live, where there's a great bar scene on Varick, but she's hanging around here, in my neighborhood of shitty bungalows? Why? We're Polish. We are not Polacks, which is how they refer to us in the nicer parts of this town. She sails – she sails around flaunting it. She's got plenty to flaunt, I'll give her that. Is she some kind of high-end whore? The wife, she goes, Ask her, Stanley, what she delivers for two dollars. I'll start with her ankles, work my way up to the promised land. How much would that cost me?

*

She's on our North side of recent nice little bungalows. Not old ones like on the West or East side. When the Polacks and the Wops have enough dough to move on up, they come to the North side. No niggers here, but sooner or later history can't be stopped. Hope I'm dead when it happens. She sashays like a bitch by our house on Sunlit Terrace and my wife says, She's asking for it, Travis, in all her holes.

I'd like to give it to her hard, in every hole.

*

Hotel Utica sits in the center of town, not far from the Liberty Street area, where a dense pocket of African-Americans live. Mid-day. Seven men of all ages, all Black, standing on the corner. They see The Italian Stranger approaching.

They flee her.

*

Someone said, they call us Christ-killers. *Mazza Crist'* is how they say it on the East Side, where those Italian-Americans have it in for us. The Italian-Americans are losing out to the diversity moving in like a tsunami. The Puerto Ricans are moving in by the galore. Muslims, Chinese. And the Bosnians, who they say are making East Utica better with the work they put into the houses, in and out. They call themselves Bosnian-Americans. There are two types of baseball fans, okay? Yankees fans and those who wish they were. There are two types of humans, okay? Jews and non-Jews. In America people call themselves Irish-Americans, Italian-Americans, Polish-Americans. They won't accept we can be Jew hyphen Americans. I am a Jewish-American. I am a fuckin' American! Some want to be Black, some want to be Italian. Nobody wants to be a Jew, including a lot of Jews. She's here, in the South Side, where there's a lot of us. Dressed like that? If you could use the word "dressed." I'm a paranoid Jew. If you're a Jew and you're not paranoid? You're asking for it. So I admit it. I followed her at a safe distance, but my heat-seeking missile doesn't respect distance because it takes its cue from my hungers, which are diverse, including this red-headed shiksa, no less.

What was she doing here? So at one point she sits on the curb and pulls out a cigarette. I cross over the street and sit opposite her. She's smoking and looking up at the sky and blowing rings with her mouth in the position of – you know darn well what I'm saying about the smoke-blowing position of her mouth. I stoop over and make believe I'm tying a loose shoe lace, which I do with quick glances in her direction, her legs wide open sitting on the curb blowing rings. Wide open, I can't see it, but I can imagine it. What's she got in her shoulder purse? A tape recorder if I strike up a conversation? She was asking for it and I hope she received it, but not from me. I'm innocent. I almost feel sorry for her. With that delicious mouth. She knew I didn't need to tie my shoe. So I glance up with a why-don't-we-get-it-on stare. G dash D, she's good looking. She smiles and shakes her head. Stands up and flicks the cigarette in my direction. Cunt.

*

She toured Utica's neighborhoods, stopping frequently to stare because she needed to see what it looked like – America's fabled diversity in this nation of immigrants and their progeny. She saw only Americans – mostly white, and unlike her countrymen not friendly and not attractive. Not attractive, she thought, because not friendly.

A self-described "witness" called Utica PD. His statement made its way to the Chief, who made one phone call. The Chief speaks. The Chief listens to the Chief of Chiefs. They chuckle. And that was that.

2.

The Uticans

His name is Rocco DiCastro – often called The Godfather, but he's just one of the dopes, as the crew of guys like to refer to one another, who work for the small city of Utica, New York, and are assigned to the maintenance of streets and parks. In summer, rather than ride a tractor, The Godfather chooses to push a rusty lawn mower across vast spaces of bumpy park green, where boys who cannot afford proper gloves play a special version of baseball, four on a side. In winter, at night, in subfreezing temperatures and slashing wind, he shovels sand and rock salt onto icy roads from the open bed of a pick-up truck, whose driver must fight off sleep to avoid veering into a culvert, overturning and killing the shoveling dopes in the open bed.

They call him The East Utica Whirlwind. They call him Big Rocky, who stands 5-5, 130 pounds. They hail him as The Earl of Eagle Street, where he lives with The Godmother on the second floor of a two-family house – accessed only by a cruelly steep and winding stair. Wonder Wop, The Golden Dago, The Rock of Ages, they call him – who plays Santa Claus for their grandchildren, and whose secret desire is to be called The Assassin.

All of the guys in the crew are godfathers, Catholics all, but he's the only one they call godfather. His nicknames, too numerous to be listed here, are spoken only with affection because Rocco DiCastro is thought to be a man without malice. His crewmates love him, though these men, being men, would never say the word that they had spoken only infrequently, with some embarrassment, long ago to their long-gone mothers, but never to their fathers.

It shall never be known how she happened to be there – this Italian Woman, this Actual Italian – there precisely in his path as he, dripping sweat in humid August, pushed well beyond the centerfielder whose mitt was one of his grandmother's torn gardening gloves. The Godfather stops. The Godfather steps in front of his mower. The Italian Woman seems to him afloat over grass. Perhaps she is. The Godfather knows female beauty. Because isn't The Godmother the most beautiful woman in the city of Utica? In the county of Oneida? And doubtless beyond? How tall, how alive this stranger is. His wife of many decades, The Godmother, creator of legendary calzones, stands 5-3 in shoes. Suddenly now a new lurch of desire. At Rocky's age? (What does age have to do with it?)

A shout from one of the players cuts the silence between them: "Hey, Frankie! You stink!" He approaches her without wanting to approach her. She – whose face says she is a pre-pubescent teenager, though she is not – does she see him, who has come so close? Her eyes are emptied of the present, as if she sees only far backward in time. A ball is struck high and deep over the centerfielder's head. The ball rolls to a stop between them. She picks it up. Pure white and unmarked. She cradles and caresses it in both hands. She says, "I wish to talk. Do you wish to talk?"

*

It's the night of their first day home from a week of honeymoon at Niagara Falls and he's struggling to watch her shower through the frosted glass door. She emerges. She begins to towel off. She says, "Want to do this for me?" He says, "No. I want to be the towel."

On the rug alongside the shower, Connie O'Donnell and Richie Romano. Richie the towel. Richie the straddled man. Connie whispers, "She ate you all up."

"Who?"

"Pretending you don't know I refer to the Italian we met at your godparents?"

"How about we –"

"Thinking about her arouses you again? So soon?"

"Your hand, Connie. Here."

"Here, Rich. You found her attractive? Here, Rich. Yes. There. There."

*

Friends had urged fashionable Hawaii, but these two old-fashioned youngsters wanted Niagara Falls, Honeymoon Capitol of the World, where their parents had celebrated decades before. At Niagara Falls she said, "honeymoan." Many years later, at breakfast, their son about to finish college, Richie would claim the pun as his own and she would reply, "You were the trigger, but the pun was mine. Potatoes with your eggs?"

On that first day back from Niagara Falls they had taken early dinner at The Chesterfield, followed by espresso (anisette-spiked) and homemade almond cookies at Richie's godparents, Rocky and Rose DiCastro. They met there a stranger from Italy, introduced by Godfather Rocky as his "cousin's sister-in-law's best friend." A member of the extended family, Italian style. She called herself Maria Silvestri.

*

Richie's about to leave to re-open Café Romano – his first child – when she says, apropos of nothing, "How could you not find her attractive? This Silvestri bitch?"

Richie, traditional Italian male, has seared himself with Connie-centered jealousy, but always unspoken. Once, even at Niagara Falls. But Connie? Jealous? Who said, when he asked if she ever was, "Unlike you, Big Rich, I don't have the jealousy-gene." Her response had troubled him. Still does. Is he so lacking in animal magnetism?

He says, "When I come home at noon –"

"For a quickie and lunch?"

"The quickie's all the lunch I'll need. Gotta run. Rosario wants to talk."

"Rosario? Martello?"

"The one and only."

"Behind his back, Rich. Remember? In high school? They called him The Altar Boy."

"How could I forget?"

"Behind his back they called him Jesus, Mary, and Joseph. He wanted to be known as Russell. God only knows why."

"We called him Russell, which no one else did. We made him happy."

"Pathetic Rosario had a thing for me, Rich, which everyone knew. Except you."

"I knew."

"You knew?"

"I still know, Connie. I'll always know."

"Always? Meaning what, exactly?"

"Did I say always?"

"You know you did, Rich."

"Here's what I know, Connie. Rosario's pathetic no more."

"I heard the rumors. So. Do you or don't you find this Silvestri attractive?"

"She's the coldest good-looking bitch I ever saw."

"You agree. You find her attractive."

"Check out my bird books."

"Why? You have so many. Which one?"

"Doesn't matter which. Any close-up of a hawk face. The eyes. The hooked beak for tearing. That's who she is."

"With an elegant model's body – except she has tits that protrude. Rich, she'll eventually tear my flesh."

He slides his hand inside the front of her pajama bottoms. He says, "Noon for a nooner, if my dick hasn't fallen off before then."

She says, "How about leaving it here – this jumping thing in my hand?"

He will not tell her that he finds hawks thrilling, as they soar high up in great lazy circles – suddenly plunging, with razor claws striking, gashing.

*

Richie took her in, of course he did, this Maria Silvestri, this Italian stranger who looked like someone he had seen before. But who? Then he knew. She looked like – exactly like the girl in the painting that his poetry teacher at Proctor High had framed behind his desk. A massive reproduction, four feet wide by six feet high. Venus standing on a something or other. He forgets by who. Probably some Italian. Long wavy red hair (like Connie), slim and tall (like Connie) and small-breasted (unlike Connie). Maria Silvestri was struck by the animal magnetism he never knew he had. The mere thought that she was attracted causes the pleasure of a stirring in his crotch. In his Godparents' kitchen, over coffee, he imagined, in a quickly disappearing image, how delicious it would be to return the favor and eat her all up – her small breasts filling his mouth to the brim.

That night on the rug alongside the shower, who really did he make love to as he exploded inside Connie? Connie herself? Maria Silvestri? Venus? Did it matter who? An extra-marital affair one week after marriage – in the mind, where it is hottest.

*

As he approaches Café Romano he sees, standing under the awning, the woman – in white, her back to the entrance, staring out at the street. And a man in dark aviator glasses, on this hot, overcast morning, turned toward the woman, speaking to her, who does not respond.

Richie says, "Russell!" Richie nods to the woman. The woman is the Italian stranger.

Richie turns the key as Russell says, "I have a surprise for you –" as he pats the bulging interior breast pocket of his sport coat. For a split second Richie thinks, What have I ever done to Rosario Martello to deserve a bullet in the brain?

The woman who calls herself Maria Silvestri takes the table closest to the front door. Russell proceeds to the table closest to Richie's passage to the kitchen. Richie asks what he can get for her on the house: "May I offer you cappuccino and a pasticciotto? Chocolate or vanilla?"

She says, "No. Only to talk."

He says, "Let me take care of the gentleman and I'll be back for a chat." (Russell has never been referred to as a gentleman.)

She says, "No. Not to chat. To talk."

He goes to Rosario, a.k.a. Russell, who keeps his aviator shades on. Russell places a thin, letter-sized envelope on the table. And a pouch: thick, bellied out. He pushes the thin envelope to Rich. It bears Rich's full name written across the front in lyrical cursive.

Russell says, "In high school it was the only thing about me you could call beautiful. My handwriting. This Richie," tapping the thin envelope, "my appreciation for how you and that heartthrob Connie treated me in high school. You never knew I had a heartbreaking crush on your wife back in the day, but I was too shy to try anything. You are a heartthrob yourself, you s.o.b. You made your irresistible move, which I never resented, as the Lord clearly knows. You two were ripe peaches when everyone else became sour grapes on behalf of my mouth. They called me 'Rose.' They called me 'Rosie.' May my parents R.I.P. for giving me that name. God willing you keep it in your pants except on the home front."

Rich says, "Those massive crushes? They never go away. They're painfully nourished forever. Because they're heartbreaking."

Russell pulls off his shades. Stares at Rich. Says, "What in God's good name are you insinuating? My good friend?" Puts his shades back on.

"What I'm saying, Russell, we always loved you. Including who you call my heartthrob wife. You can take it to the bank."

"This is love and the bank, Rich –" as he pushes the fat pouch across the table. "Untraceable cold cash. From The Falcon himself."

"I'm speechless, Russ." (Speechless because he has been long indebted to The Falcon.)

"On behalf of The Falcon I sincerely advise keep it that way. In the future, starting now, it's 'Russell' – never 'Russ.' I prefer the formality. Sincerely advise you keep that in mind."

"My lips are sealed, Russell."

"Don't turn around, Rich. She's staring at you in the back. You know who she is?"

"Maria Silvestri."

"That name? A detour away from the depths. In other words, the razor blade hiding between her upper thighs. Don't turn around. She's a statue looking into your back."

"You know something I don't?"

"Know what I cherish about you, Mr. Richard Romano? You always understood my requirements. People come in here, they order cannoli, you bring how many?"

"Two."

"Par for the course in this establishment. I never ask, you bring me how many?"

"Three."

"Which you haven't done yet. By the way."

"You want your three cannolis?"

"Too late. You missed the protocol. What was the conversation like at Rocky's and Rosie's?"

"The one from Italy says, How many live in Utica? I tell her 110,000. She says, How many Italians? I tell her about 40,000. She says, Born in Italy. Not the ones born here who call themselves Italians. Who are Americans. I tell her fewer every year. Like my grandparents. She says, Your grandparents."

"What does your knockout wife think of her?"

"She didn't like – in fact, I'd say –"

"Connie wants her off the calendar, Rich?"

"I don't think Connie would go that far."

"How far is far, Richard?"

"You know, Russell."

"Better believe I know. So do you. Shall we stop this pussy-fingering? The Falcon is the King of Far. At the beginning of our relationship The Falcon says, Russell, I know from my daughter how they mocked you with the name The Altar Boy. You're going to be my Altar Boy. A-L-T-E-R. Then those that mocked you will fear you. They will nod with respect as they pass you on the street. They will pick up your check wherever you dine. They will want you to like them. What else did the Italian woman have to say?"

"When you go to Italy," she says, "stand close to the Bay of Naples and smell the rotting flesh."

Russell makes the sign of the cross.

"Nobody says a word. We're having coffee and Rosie's –"

"Homemade almond cookies."

"How did you know, Russell?"

"Rosie understands my hair. She's been cutting it for years. We talk. She and The Falcon's mother go back. Guess who taught The Falcon to drive years ago? Rosie. He calls her his *consigliere*. You follow? He loves her. Just like you and Rosie, it's a godmother, godson type thing. I tell her I never had a godmother. She goes, Russell, I am your substitute godmother forever."

"Funny my godmother never mentioned – she's The Falcon's godmother?"

"Your godmother has inner sides. Let's leave it at that."

"Russell, my Italian is lousy. What is *consigliere*? Do I want to know?"

"Counselor. In all matters. Especially grave matters." (He laughs.) "Matters of the grave." (He laughs.) "Any reactions after the Italian visitor drops the rotting flesh bomb?"

"Rocky goes white. Connie says, More coffee, anyone? No one answers. I give my godmother a look, who gives the visitor a look that to me says, Who is my godmother, really, after all these years?"

"Don't turn around, Rich. The Italian statue is staring right into your heart."

"Should I fear her? Should Connie?"

"Remember that skinny little pisser in our senior year who liked to lean on my car? Where did he get off? I guarantee I never intended to paralyze him for life."

"Russell, Connie and me – we never thought you intended to paralyze –"

"Paralysis, Rich. Unintended. Irreversible. Tell the Italian visitor that story."

"Hang around for awhile, Russell. Maria Silvestri wants to talk."

"Maria Romano just walked out."

Richie turns to see the empty chair: "You mean Maria Silvestri. Silvestri."

"I mean Maria Romano. Romano."

"She wanted to – 'Romano' you're calling her? Possibly related to –?"

"Everything is possible. She left a note."

Richie retrieves the note. Russell says, "What's it say?"

"I can't read Italian. Can you?"

"Nothing except '*va fare in culo.*' Did she write those words?"

"Only word I recognize, possibly, is *amanti*. Possibly related to love. Godmother Rosie will translate."

"Speaking of Rosie, you and Connie need to know something about this so-called Silvestri."

"What?"

"Not at liberty to say."

"When we leave my godparents, Russell, this Italian says to me, Do you know the great Renaissance painter, the underrated Giulio

Romano? I say, My grandfather, Giulio Romano, once painted his bathroom and made a disaster. Oh, she says, your grandfather is also named Giulio Romano?"

"Like she didn't know, Rich. Like she didn't know."

*

Russell Martello pushes his shades up to his forehead. Richie averts his eyes from the Martello death stare and looks abruptly down at Russell's shoes, with no interest in Russell's shoes. The socks. One black, the other a yellowed orange. Richie suppresses a smile. Is this hit man sending a message to the queer edge of the current generation?

Russell says, "The Lord knows I need to move my bowels," though he (Martello, like The Lord) does not, as he walks with awkward gait to the rest room, a man in his mid-20s, wearing a catheter. Time to empty the bag of its yellow-orange fluid. When he returns he says, "Richie, my pretty urologist recommends a needle in the balls. May sweet baby Jesus forgive the vernacular."

*

"What did you say, Grandma?"

"GODmother, Joey Furillo. Not grandma. GODmother."

"What did you say, Grandgod?"

"*Diavolo! La vita é amara.* Life is bitter."

"Godmother, what is butter?"

Rose DiCastro had prepared the moment. "Bitter, not butter. Like this," handing him a slice of lemon peel. "Chew," she says. "Chew."

He chews and instantly spits it out. He says, "Give me a cannoli."

She does. She says, "All of life, *diavolo*, is bitterness you cannot spit out."

He says, "Give me another cannoli. I want another one now!" He has not yet finished eating the first one.

The Godmother says, "We have only one more. We must save it for Godfather Rocky, when he comes home from work."

Joey, four-year-old Joey, says, "Give it to me now or I will kick you in the BALLS!"

She pauses. She nods. She smiles tightly. She says, "Bravissimo, Joey," and gives him the last cannoli.

He says, "Grandgod, now I will not kick you in the balls."

At four, Joey Furillo fathers the man that he will become. To be feared across all of the Upstate New York – from north of Albany to the Canadian border, from east of Albany to the border of Vermont, and from northwest of Albany to Buffalo and the edge of Pennsylvania. Joey Furillo will ascend to the place occupied by the apex bird of prey and become known as Don Joseph (The Falcon) Furillo. Spoken of, when spoken of at all, only as The Falcon, *sotto voce*.

*

Five-year-old Richie watched him working in the garden beneath the cherry tree, which had been permitted to grow far beyond its natural self. Higher than his two-story house and wider than – who knows how wide? The man in the garden is Giulio Romano, Big Giulio as he is known at the Catholic cemetery in Utica, where he's been employed since he arrived in America, after sailing into New York Harbor from the Bay of Naples in 1909. Planting trees, trimming around the grave stones, mowing in the long green aisles and digging once weekly – excavating in stubborn, pebble-infested soil – six feet deep, eight long, three and a half wide. What it took two ordinary mortals of able body eight hours to achieve he did alone in three.

For his epical feats of strength and endurance they call him Big Giulio, who stands 5'9", 165 pounds – as Richie Romano watches him, his paternal grandfather – hawk-nosed and bald and ignoring the transfixed child who says, "Grandpa, what did you do in It'ly?" And Big Giulio responding by picking a tomato, dipping it into the cold water of the rain barrel, drying it on his shirt (heavy flannel in humid 80 degree weather), taking a bite and handing it to the boy, and saying in Italian that Richie cannot understand, "Not necessary, the olive oil. Not necessary the salt. Eat." And Richie Romano eats and the juices run down from the corners of his grinning mouth as he says, once again, "Grandpa, what did you do in It'ly?"

THE FALCONS OF DESIRE

Richie would ask countless times, but would receive no answer until he was 16, when Big Giulio decided to tell him the nasty truth in appropriately nasty language, in his limited English: "Shovel shit in the cow barn of the padrone." Richie was ignorant of the extreme poverty and aristocratic contempt that drove out the immigrants from their homes in the south of Italy – their huts of one room with dirt floors. He wanted to know why his grandfather did what he did in the Old Country and Big Giulio answered in Italian, of which Richie would always be mostly ignorant: "Still? (*Ancora?*) You have sixteen years and you are still (*ancora*) a cucumber?"

*

When Giulio Romano, owner of the house at 1303 Mary Street, is forced to assisted living, Richie Romano – proprietor of a lucrative café, who could have lived in Utica's exclusive suburb – offers to buy the house. But Giulio would accept no money and instead deeded 1303 to Richie, who spent his Sundays "in the garden of my grandfather," as he thought of it. Or sitting on the corner fence with the old Italians, who would not move out of the Lower East Side because they were deep-rooted trees.

In the heart of working class Italian-American East Utica, the house at 1303 Mary Street can be found just above the east-west thoroughfare called Bleecker: a 20 minute walk west to the café on Bleecker, which Richie undertakes six days a week – absorbing each day, as if for the first time, the sparrows hopping in the gutter, the fish market, the green market, the emaciated feral cat, the barber shop, the meat market, the six bakeries and those women who lean from third-story windows (always the same two) on each side of Bleecker, as they scream to each other above the racket of children on the sidewalk and the roar of the buses, which Richie will never board. What he sees along the way, he inhales – including the three-legged dog he names Angie. What he sees and inhales is himself. At 25 Romano wants to become a tree. Though born in Utica, in his imagined self he came over on the boat from the Old Country. Richie Romano: 25 going on 75, a daily presence on Bleecker, to whom the third-story screamers call out: "Ciao! Guapo!"

Words which, sadly, he does not understand. Words that translate to Hello! Handsome!

Richard Romano imagines himself Italian-born, he who knows little Italian.

*

They live on the same street – same block – three houses between them. The Professor and The Falcon. They have never spoken – even when passing each other on their customary early morning strolls, The Professor with his leashed pit bull, The Falcon with his enforcer, the unleashed Rosario ("Russell") Martello, who attempts now on this pivotal day to take The Falcon's arm, as if they were a long-married Old World couple – and The Falcon rebuffing Martello with a backhanded slap and a muttered Italian obscenity, best not cited here, much less translated. Until this morning, The Professor and The Falcon have acknowledged each other silently with polite, meaningless nods and the smallest of tight smiles.

The Professor is Utica's bright Star of Intelligence, thanks to having won a Rhodes Scholarship many years ago. Whenever he enters Café Romano, the gathered regulars, ball-busters all, call out with affection, Here he comes! The Rhodes Scholar! As they spell Rhodes R-O-A-D-S. Don Furillo, Utica's Mafia Star of Black Light, has never been the subject of open mockery in person – the ball-busters lack the balls – or even been mocked quietly when far out of earshot – or even mocked in the fantasy world of their minds, where the mockers tremble at the thought of who he is – as he slithers into the burrow of a defenseless rabbit and proceeds, teeth-bared, directly to the eyes, then meat, organs, bones, fur and, most deliciously, the feces-swollen intestines.

Within a few feet of one another, The Professor stops. The Falcon, with a stare, does as well. The Professor says, "Don Furillo, I can no longer abide our silence. May I have the pleasure of a private audience?" The Falcon says, "This person, Russell, not only he reads a lot of books, he talks like one. You want private? You sure? Don't answer too fast. Think." The Professor says, "Yes, sir. Private, sir." The Falcon says, "Let us repair, then, to my kitchen, as they say on Downtown Anthony. I got a leaky faucet. Can you repair it? Russell here repairs my external leaks, but not those in the house. You a plumber in your spare time? Don't make me laugh." The Professor says, "I am capable of repairing your faucet, among other matters of the house, though not of the marital kind." The Falcon says, "You implicating about me and the wife?" The Professor says, "No, sir. Never." Martello says, "Prof, anybody at the fuckin' college bothering you? Just give me their name and address."

*

At the Falcon's door The Falcon says, "No filth enters, Russell. Fresh socks this morning? Or the ones from yesterday, which you left smelly last night next to your bed? I don't want to think about when you last changed the sheets." Russell assures The Falcon that his socks are fresh. The Falcon says, "Talk to me, Professor." The Professor says, "Fresh. This morning." The Falcon says, "The vicious dog stays here. If he loves you, he'll wait." The Falcon opens the door, "The both of you, take off your shoes and go in." The Falcon says, "Russell. You know the drill." Russell places them at the threshold. The Falcon removes his shoes and steps daintily into his fluffy white slippers.

*

The three of them walk into the kitchen at 7:45 to find The Falcon's wife in the midst of forking down maple syrup drowned pancakes, piled high. She stands immediately, saying, "Joe, you know this is the thing you promised to spare me the knowledge of it." The Falcon says to Russell, "Take the Pig of Pancakes to the mall, where she is happy." Russell says, "They don't open until 10." The Falcon says, "All of a sudden you hard of hearing? The mall."

*

The Falcon says, "My daughter loves your Jewlysses class on Joyce and because of you she didn't come home last night. She told me she was visiting Nighttown, which according to her is part of Joyce's book. I tell her, and now you, I don't want to talk about Nighttown, whatever it is, which I can guess. You got your mutual privacy. Talk to me. You want cappuccino? No? I myself don't drink Italian coffee or otherwise. You want herbal tea? No? Me either. Talk to me, Professor. Life is shorter than you think."

The Professor of Literature at Utica College pours out a story of being punched and kicked by a minor Utica bully and Mafia wannabe, who The Don scorns because the violence that the wannabe does is motiveless. The Professor tells him that he had intervened when Michael Caco was pushing around a 9-year-old boy on the playground when Caco was 18 – and Caco had turned on him for doing so. The Falcon says, "I don't see on your face what you claim he did. How come?" The Professor says, "I want him to suffer as I have suffered." The Falcon says, "When did it happen? Spit it out. You don't look beat up in the least." The Professor says, "Many years ago." The Falcon says, "I learned in my profession you don't wait too long. You act without mercy inside a month. Beyond a month you brood, you get an ulcer, you get heart trouble. Then you destroy yourself. You took a chance when you put your hands in someone else's filth. Professor, stop strangling yourself with piano wire, as they say in certain fields of expertise. This Caco, in case you haven't heard, is tied down to a wheelchair and an oxygen machine for the last 6 months. He's in a shithole where he belongs, which he'll never escape. You're in a mental shithole, which you're the blame for it. Don't contradict me. You want to get out? Flush the past. I will not intervene."

The Professor says, "I am happy to reimburse you handsomely for your services." The Falcon says, "My craft is not for sale for a headcase who should talk to a psychiatrist. You say you want him to suffer as I have suffered. I saw that movie. Actors pretend, my friend. I do not pretend." The Professor cannot speak. The Falcon says, "Shall we change the subject?" The Professor says, "Please."

The Falcon: "What is Joyce's last name? My daughter talks about Jane. She talks about Emily. She talks about Virginia. Now thanks to you it's Joyce morning, noon, and night. Joyce. What's Joyce's last name?"

The Professor: "Actually, how shall I say this … James is actually –"

The Falcon: "Joyce James? JJ? Like the JJ of my broken heart? The JJ of my youth? I am referring to Joni James of Chicago, where I have serious friends. She was an Italian for your information. She had to change her name because they wouldn't say Giovanna Carmella Babbo on the radio in the early days of television. Imagine Ed Sullivan saying her true name? [He croons] Why don't you believe me? / I love only you / Here is a heart that is lonely / Here is a heart that is blue / Here is a heart for you only / That you can keep or break! ... Professor, can Joyce James sing like Joni? Nobody can."

The Professor: "Actually, Joyce had a sweet tenor voice. He sang Italian arias when he was unhappy."

The Falcon: "Tenor?! What are you insinuating, Professor? This Joyce is one of those switcheroo females? Does my daughter know this? She is a big feminine theologist. Are you, Professor, a big feminine theologist?"

The Professor: "No, but if I were, I could do worse."

The Falcon: "Worse? Like two in the back of your head?"

The Professor: "Yes, sir. That would be –"

The Falcon: "Shall we change the topic? I don't enjoy dwelling on two in the back of your black curly head. Do you know the songs of Joni James?"

The Professor: "Afraid not. Before my time."

The Falcon: "Afraid? What are you afraid of? [croons] You're my everything. You should know that one. Oh my God! [croons] Don't tell me not to love you. Professor! [croons] There must be a way – that one, Professor, There must be a way because Joni and I never had a way. In my secret life I was a lonely heart. I had nothing but desire for Joni, which means I had nobody as Joni sang [croons] There goes my heart. She understood me in the early morning hours, at dawn when she sang [croons] I woke up crying. Who is Joni, you're thinking? Joni is love."

The Professor: "When you sing, sir, I hear not only her heart-crushing songs, I hear Joni herself. Smooth, melancholy, and sultry – and you, you are Joni, as you carry me from this harsh world to a beautiful place which no longer exists. From you, her voice pours like a river, it comes forth like endless, unbroken sound, as if she never takes a breath. You gave me a past I never had. You gave me Joni James. You,

Don Joseph, are the miracle of her incarnation."

The Falcon: "You blaspheme! You are ill!"

The Professor: "Forgive me, Don Joseph, for I know not what I say."

The Falcon: "I never forgot Joni, even after I got together with my so-called wife, who loves only the mall. That is Teresa. The mall-fucker. I hate her from the bottom of my heart, where I cook cesspool dinners for all who displease me. One day I say to Teresa, Teresa, dear, eat shit and die. You are extremely sick, Prof, but you please me greatly and I am going to make this Caco suffer on your behalf. With his oxygen mask on, in his wheelchair, sitting in piss and shit, he will beg for death like it's his mother's fat, flowing tit."

*

The Godmother, connoisseur of Hollywood movies of the 40s and 50s, believes that mouth-watering noir-star Dana Andrews, long dead, inhabits the body of Dominic the Butcher. The difference, Dom is sexier than Dana, with a fuller face, as if he, Dom, has just finished bedding his sixth wife: lips parted, his face swollen in blood-engorged orgasmic aftermath, at all hours of the day, like now, as he, Dom, reaches into the display case to retrieve ground chuck for her meatballs – "not the tasteless fat-free atrocity favored by enlightened liberals, too liberal to take their own side in a fight unto death, but fat-veined ground chuck for big balls, Rose," says Dom, "which we add a little water or they become rocks." Thinks Rose, like Rocky's balls, even at his age. The Godmother says, "And chops, Dom." "Pork?" he says. "Always," she says, "and those Italian sausages, those nice long ones." Dom says, "Shall I cut them in half?" "No, Dom, out of respect to the sausage I eat it whole." So Rose to the giggling and barrel-chested butcher.

He gives her three packages: one each for the ground chuck, the pork chops, and the six long sausages. On each package, with a sharpie, he writes: NO CHARGE. No matter what she buys, or how much she buys, when she wheels her cart to the check-out counter she is greeted by the cashier with the same gesture for the last seven years. A wave of the hand. "Go on, Mrs. DiCastro, your money is not required here at the Chicago Market. Have a beautiful day, beautiful."

Seven years ago, on an icy February morning in the parking lot of the Chicago Market, The Godmother runs over and kills Alderman Roger (The Dumb Polack) Postucki, mayor wannabe, who had proposed the week before "a resolution with teeth to rid our fair city of the scourge of organized crime." The Dumb Polack didn't need to mention the name Don Joseph Furillo. When questioned by Detective Angelo Buono, Rose states, "I'm pulling out of my parking spot with my groceries on the back seat and this man who at the time I don't know who he is, he all of the sudden falls down and slides under my car. What could I do? It was a tragedy, Angelo, that deprived our city of this great fighter against corruption. Ang, tell me, how's Angelina? Give her my love from here to eternity, starring the delicious Burt Lancaster, the iceberg Deborah Kerr, Montgomery Clift, who is also delicious, and Frank Sinatra, who is too short to be delicious – not to mention Ernest Borgnine, who I could never swallow. Give Angelina my love. Ang?"

"Yes, Rose?"

"Ang, we're done here."

*

One week before the Senior Ball and Marianna Furillo has no date. What senior male in his right mind would ask her? Who had not already dated her several times in the parking lot of Proctor High, where she would be found waiting in her Mercedes, seven nights per week? Or on any late afternoon, after the last class, waiting again in the parking lot, in the gleaming Mercedes, where Thunder Thighs, who will not go all the way, administers head to the boys who had heard erection-inducing rumors of such a thing and came to climax in 1.47 seconds.

No boy has ever knocked on Marianna's front door, at the appointed hour, to be greeted by her mother. Or, God forbid, by her father – The Falcon himself.

One week before the Ball, a senior male, who has himself never had a proper date, has no option. Rosario Martello – this routinely scorned object of the graduating class – Rosario Martello, spouter of religious rhetoric, suddenly sees, three days before the Ball, his path to a future of respect, financial comfort, and chilling power. So he awaits her exit from Spanish 1A and greets her when she does with a gift-wrapped box of chocolates. She says, "No way, buster. I got an upset stomach and can't swallow your injection this afternoon, if that's your big idea." Rosario says, "Marianna, Marianna, I'm asking you to the Ball, not the parking lot. If you refuse me, The Good Lord knows you will break my heart."

She tells her mother, who tells The Falcon, who says, "This is the kid I read about in the paper? Who paralyzed a classmate for life, for understandable reasons?" Marianna says, "Your type, daddy." The Falcon says, "He's gonna knock on my front door? A first." Her mother says, "Let's be grateful, Joe. She's never going to be our quiet Rosemary. This nice boy gave her a box of Fanny Farmer in advance. This is a very nice boy."

On the night of the Senior Ball Rosario Martello appears at the front door in a tuxedo, bearing in each hand a dozen roses – one for Marianna, the other for her mother. The Falcon has an eye for rare talent and sees, immediately, in Martello's eyes, the appealing deadness.

Two days after the Ball, The Falcon brings Rosario on board. To run innocent errands. ("A carton of Camel Lights.") To hand deliver unsigned letters. To issue, orally, interesting suggestions.

Rosario marries Marianna, who is run over and killed by a bus as she jaywalks on Bleecker – her head exploded under the massive double wheels, on the morning after the night, in bed, when she had yet once more denied the hopelessly tumescent Rosario the oral sex she had once granted to all who applied. Rosario had refrained from requesting the act until their wedding night, when he was rebuffed, as he was rebuffed ever since. She said on the night before her last day on earth, "Do I have to remind you? Again? As a married individual I am no longer required to go to the lower level."

When Rosario was given the news of her gruesome death, he exclaimed, in the presence of the flunky who had informed him, "Mother of God!" Then added in the same breath, "Sweet Jesus! Let her suck on THAT!" The blameless bus driver disappears a week later – his car found in a neighboring village, with a broad urine stain on the driver's seat.

Widower Rosario continued to do his chores for The Falcon, until The Falcon made him an offer for a quadrupled weekly salary and a ranch-style home of his own, free of charge, in Utica's expensive Upper East Side, which he would earn by neutralizing a Syrian immigrant who was cutting into The Falcon's pie. The conversation at 2 am in the Don's deep backyard goes this way: "I want this Syrian cocksucker alive and healthy and forking over 80% of his earnings. I want him sent a message through his gorgeous wife. I need a man of brass balls. Are you the man?" Rosario answers, "Don Joseph, may The Lord strike me dead if I am not the man."

One week later, the gorgeous wife is found coughed up in the polluted Mohawk River – shot and partially disemboweled, Utica's 30th unsolved murder in The Falcon's reign. Thus did Rosario Martello earn the meaning of his surname and become, at last, The Hammer.

On the day before his wife's burial, the Syrian mobster finds in his mailbox an anonymous note: How much do you love your tasty three-year-old daughter?

*

Among the dark-haired, olive-toned and brown-eyed of Italian descent at Proctor High, on Utica's East Side – called Dago Town in other parts of the city – there once moved a compelling alien: a redheaded and blue-eyed beauty of alabaster complexion named Connie O'Donnell, who triggered the usual reactions. Desire among many of the males and some few females and ill-wishes among more than a few females, especially after she blossomed as the whirling point guard of the girls' basketball team. Connie O'D, she was called by her coach and team mates – feared by opposing players for the brutal picks that she set, one of which resulted in a badly sprained shoulder (hers) which she did not disclose and for which she did not seek medical attention until after the state championship game, when she rescued Proctor by snatching a rebound from a taller and stronger player and flying down the length of the floor to score the winning shot, with a fraction of a second remaining on the game clock. Thereafter she was celebrated in the student newspaper and the city daily as "*il diavolo rosso*," the red devil, whose smile was the risen sun for Proctor's shy and depressed – students, staff and faculty alike – who all walked the school's halls with fixed downward gazes, except when she was coming their way.

One month after the end of the basketball season, near the conclusion of her sophomore year, she performed to acclaim as Pegeen Mike, the female lead in *The Playboy of the Western World*. Connie O'Donnell disappeared and became Pegeen Mike. At the outset of her Junior year, her classmates – though seeing her physical form moving in Proctor's halls – could not locate the person they had known as Connie O'Donnell. She had been, just a few months before, Pegeen Mike. Who was she now?

The smile is gone. She passes them in the halls but sees nothing. Is she thinking? Imagining? What? Gone crazy? The cheerleader coach wanted her to lead the squad. Flatly, without a trace of heat, Connie said, "Fuck cheer. Basketball. Drama Club. Fuck Proctor, Coach Kozlowski. Italian food is overrated. Kielbasa is my thing," she says to the svelte divorcee of Polish extraction, who spends two weeks each summer in Krakow with thick Polish sausage, Kielbasa, on her mind.

Connie takes a small beribboned blue box from her jacket. She says to Coach Kozlowski, "This is for you." The Coach opens it to find a necklace resembling no necklace she has ever seen. Resembling no necklace no one has ever seen. The coach says, "Thank you, but I cannot accept such an expensive gift." Connie says, "I didn't buy it. I made it. Free for you." Coach K says, "I would like to buy one for my daughter." Connie says, "You can't. This is one of a kind. Like all my work." Coach K says, "But you could make a copy if you wanted to." Connie says, "I don't want to."

Coach K says, "Does it have a name?"

Connie says, "Would you like it to have one?"

Coach K says, "Yes."

Connie says, "How about, *Beauty – Take it or Leave it?*"

*

As the Italian stranger who calls herself Maria leaves Café Romano and walks east along Bleecker, men walking in the opposite direction, on her side of the street, shy sharply from her path. Her destination – and perhaps destiny – is 1303 Mary Street, Richie's house, where Connie has decided to delay her morning shower until just before 12, when Richie returns for the much-anticipated nooner. Connie in her pajamas dusts the furniture, which does not need dusting. She's just killing time. She will not change out of her pajamas. What would be the point of changing out of her pajamas before her shower? Now vacuuming the rugs, which do not need vacuuming, when the doorbell cuts through the roar of the vacuum cleaner. Big Rich? Already? Undone by passion and couldn't wait until noon? Why would he ring the doorbell? Playing the dangerous male coming to ravage me? She unbuttons her pajama top to reveal cleavage and opens the door to a woman in white, Maria, who says to speechless Connie, "I am grateful that you have prepared properly for my arrival. I smile. You do not. Why not?" Connie manages, "I thought you were …" as she fumbles and fails to button her pajama top. The Italian Stranger says, "Your handsome mate is at the Café talking with a man he fears and you must fear too," as she reaches over and buttons Connie's pajama top and so very gently grazes, and graces, Connie O'Donnell's flesh.

Maria Silvestri says, "I have desired to talk with your husband's godfather, and to your husband himself, concerning the true reason I come to your city. But absurd to talk with men concerning this. Here in the heat like Napoli, I feel the chill, but you … so warm to my finger. Will you invite me to enter? To talk of my reason understood by women everywhere?"

"You serious, Silvestri?"

"Romano is my name. Silvestri I call myself to honor my grandmother. I am Silvestri until her honor is restored."

Sudden hard rain.

"Permit me, please, to enter. To talk."

"Enter? With two last names? One step. One. Don't close the door."

"Thank you."

"Don't close the door."

"I come to Utica to talk of widows. Black and white. Not race. Clothes and death. Women in black after their husbands die. In black they are until they die. Women in white until they die – their husbands all the time in another country alive and happy, in another country."

"Old Italian ladies in black are standard in this part of town. Never heard of a white widow, unless you're one in that expensive outfit. So your husband dumped you? This is my concern? I'll call you a cab."

"I come to talk of your husband's grandfather, Giulio Romano, who made a white widow, my grandmother, Maria Silvestri, his wife in Italy before he came to America. In Italy he made a son, another Giulio, who was my father. The first Giulio, your husband's grandfather, promised to his wife in Italy to return. He did not. He married again in Utica. To have another son, the father of your husband. Unlike you, I do not have a husband named Richard who will make me a white widow."

"I let you in my house to hear that? In MY house?"

"Men are born to betray. You do not know this? Your husband is a man. The grandson of bigamist Giulio Romano."

"Get out."

"The unhappiness –"

"You deaf? Leave."

"The unhappiness of Maria Silvestri brought her before the Bay of Naples, where Giulio left for the beautiful whore called America, who destroyed many women in the South of Italy. Maria Silvestri sat too many days before the Bay of Naples, waiting for his return. The sun glittering on the water – glittering even under the cover of clouds, glittering in the dark of night. She reached out to the glittering sea to grasp nothing. Destroyed on the shore of the Bay of Naples. By her own hand destroyed. Her body not discovered for six days. Rotting in the heat and eaten by flies and wild dogs."

"Get out."

"Your husband enjoyed how I looked at him. I believe that his tongue is curious."

Connie pushes her through the open door. The Italian woman falls hard in the rain. Connie locks the door. Calls Café Romano.

*

The Falcon grabs The Professor's shoulder. He massages painfully deep. He says, "You know what I heard? I heard you teach poetry."

The wincing Professor says, "Not poetry, sir. Poultry." After a long pause, still massaging, The Falcon says, "You're almost funny. Which can't save you when you go to your car and you put the key in the ignition. Follow me? You turn the key in the ignition. Follow me? Suddenly you become 500 pieces." The Professor says, "Sir, 500 sounds quite conservative." The Falcon chuckles. He says, "I like you, Professor. So far. In my personal view, my daughter deserves A plus. That your personal view?" The Professor says, "Our personal views, Don Joseph, are similar." The Falcon, massaging again, says, "Similar or the same?" The Professor, close to tears, says "You're hurting – the same ..." The Falcon withdraws his swollen-veined hand from the Professor's shoulder. The Falcon says, "Someday soon I hope to learn poultry."

*

Even before leaving The Falcon's cage, he knew what he wanted to do as he reached his desk, the site of happiness, where he had plunged for years into the writing of books that none, including his capable colleagues, could read. The book on Joyce's *Finnegans Wake* was impossible, they said. The book on Wallace Stevens, they said, was even more obscure.

At the desk of happiness, The Professor forgets himself as the alien of Utica College, where he knows himself as an East Utica dummy, who could not converse with the easy eloquence of his Ivy League-bred colleagues. His rhythm and tone and diction and overall physical demeanor, his chairwoman once said – not quite out of earshot – were those of a barely literate construction worker, who somehow had written landmark studies of avant-garde literature.

At Café Romano, which he frequents three mornings weekly, he finds no haven. The feeling there of being out of place is worse, as he sits among the guys he grew up with, none of whom went to college and who all remain forever intimate with a way of life that gives their speech sensuous vigor, which he is convinced he once had, but had lost on his semi-pleasurable hike through eight years of undergraduate and graduate training.

Wandering between the worlds of academia and Café Romano, he belongs only to the desk of self-forgetting, where the self-loathing Professor is not permitted to sit. Where he will research the life, times and art of Joni James – so much the better to draw close, this is his desire, to draw very close to the man who has given him physical pain.

*

When Richard Romano picks up the phone at the Café he hears a voice he knows to be his wife's, pouring out of a woman who cannot be his wife. The former Connie O'Donnell, as he thought of her on the way home, was immune, or so she claimed, to feelings of jealousy, as he was not. A woman self-possessed. Always. This new Connie wailed at the edge of hysteria from certainty of his imminent betrayal. "Just like your idol did – your beloved bigamist of a fucking grandfather." She had somehow intuited his desire to bed the Italian Stranger? "Like your grandfather the bigamist, this Italian cunt and you will make me a white widow." White widow? Words that meant nothing to Romano.

She meets him at the door – says nothing and returns to her work table, where the elements of her one-of-a-kind necklaces are neatly arranged, in a shape in itself artistic. She has returned, perfectly composed, to touch the materials of her art. To sink into the cool feel of textures, which never fail to transport her elsewhere, far from herself to a world of unstained beauty. There will be no nooner today and a future nooner is beyond imagination.

"White widow? What is that? Betray you with this Silvestri? Never." She would not respond. He walks to the door, turns the knob and says, "I'm going to the Hospice of St. Luke and will put this story of bigamy she peddled to you, which you bought. I'll put it directly to Giulio." She holds up to the late morning sun, streaming through the tall window, a small uniquely-shaped silver metal, and she smiles, but does not turn to her husband. He looks back. She says "Wait, Richard" – disappears and returns with a yellowing, frayed document. She says, "This is the truth of Giulio." He reads. Without comment, he leaves.

*

The Hospice of St. Luke is located in a section of the former Woolworth's building in mostly deserted downtown Utica, where the dying patients are subjected to the moans and violent sounds coming from an adjacent dental office, and the frequent cries of "Jesus! No!" out of the chiropractor's suite next to the dental office, and down the hallway, in one direction, from the dark thunder of a four-lane bowling alley and, in the other direction, from a training space the snarling and growling of impossible dogs eager to chew off the trainer's genitals.

There are beds for only seven patients, a number in recognition of the relentless and quick rate of turnover. Three nurses: one young, one middle-aged, the other so-called old. Three nurses, three types of attractive. For Grandfather Giulio, three types of irresistible. At 93 and seven months, Grandfather Giulio does not resist.

A nurse, the oldest, leaves Giulio's bedside just as Richie appears and Giulio, pointing to her, says, "*Guarda! Guarda! Che culo! Buona per mangiare.*" She stops and does not respond to the dying Giulio, whose Italian is beyond her: "Look! Look! What an ass! Good for eating!"

She says to Richie, "The old guy is on his way out, but he's a devil. Probably always was. Whenever we come to care for him, he tries to squeeze our behind and breasts. He usually succeeds. One hand on us, the other below the covers, out of sight. You know what he's doing with that hand out of sight? Do I have to spell it out with that hand under the covers? He related to you?"

"My grandfather."

"Hope to God it doesn't run in the family."

And Giulio, watching her leave the room, says again with exuberance, "*Che culo!*"

Richie pulls a chair alongside Giulio's bed. Giulio pats the bed, signaling Richie to sit. Richie complies, takes Giulio's hand, and asks, "*Come stai, nonno?*" His Italian extends not much beyond that – "How are you, Grandfather?"

Giulio responds in Italian, assuming that his cucumber grandson has finally acquired the language: "*Mezza mort!*" (Half dead.) And then, again in Italian, "Jesus! You have finally learned!"

Richie understands not a word. He smiles and nods, to cover his ignorance. He says, in English, which Giulio has much more of than Richie has of Italian, "Those nurses, Grandpa …" but cannot finish as Giulio interrupts with extreme vulgarity, in Italian, that he will, before he dies, maybe tonight, fuck them all. Again, not understanding, Richie says, "I remember when Grandma went back to visit Italy, when I was 11. But you did not go with her. She wanted to see her old village and old friends. Why didn't you? Were you too sick to go?"

Giulio pauses, and pauses, then says harshly, "*Non mi ricordo!*"

Richie says, "What?"

Giulio says it in English, "I don't remember!" And for emphasis, in Italian, adds "*Nulla! Niente!*"

Richie leaps, "Did you know someone in Italy whose name was Maria Silvestri?"

Giulio, immediately: "No! Who is she? No."

Richie, bolder: "Was she my first grandmother? Who died in Italy after you came to America?"

Giulio answers: "*America bella. Italia paese da merda.*" (Land of shit.)

Richie says, "Grandpa, before you come to this Hospice of St. Luke –"

"To die."

"You gave your important papers to me. Connie –"

"*Bella donna.*"

"She showed me your Ellis Island record. It says before you got here you were married already in Italy. To Maria Silvestri. What Ellis Island says you told them is wrong?"

Giulio pushes Richie's hand away. He says, "Not wrong."

Richie says, "That's why you didn't want to go back with Grandma? Because Maria Silvestri was possibly alive? She was there, where you left her? You gave her a child?"

Giulio takes Richie's hand again. He says, "You are intelligent."

When Richie Romano leaves the Hospice of Saint Luke, he does not see the Italian Woman standing directly across the street. Standing still, watching.

*

Godmother Rose DiCastro hangs up and moves quickly to the living room, where Godfather Rocky sits – shoulders hiked up, hunched over, eyes glued to the TV. She sits beside him.

He says, "I have tremendous anxiety."

She says, "I just got a call – we have to talk about something."

He says, "I'm in trouble."

She points to the TV and says, "Because you and those Yankees?"

"In Boston," he says. "Rose, the Yankees could lead by a hundred to nothing in the ninth inning, but in Boston it does not matter. The Yankees lose, guaranteed, in late September, when first place is at stake."

She massages the back of his neck.

He says, "I hate Boston."

She says, "On your behalf, Rock, I also hate Boston."

He says, "Thank you."

She continues to massage his neck, as they sit quietly, watching the Yankees expand the lead to 19-1.

She rises and switches off the TV.

He protests, "I need to hear the post-game analysis. The detailed review of Boston's humiliation in Boston."

"I just got off the phone with Richie. We need to do something about her. Someone has to do something. Without mercy."

"About who?" he says.

"This Italian Woman. Who we introduced to Richie and Connie. Maria so-called Silvestri, whose real name is Romano, according to Richie."

"This is a crisis?"

"The story I just got from Richie, he's coming home for lunch today. Connie is still in her pajamas waiting for him with the buttons of her top unbuttoned down to her –"

"Don't spell it out, Rose, unless you're trying to rile me up. Lunch before lunch at noon. I get it."

"But someone gets there *before* Richie does."

"Who?"

"Maria so-called Silvestri."

"Out of the blue she drops in on Connie?"

"Without warning she drops in and tells Connie that Giulio

was married in Italy before he immigrated. To Maria Silvestri. The grandmother of this so-called Maria Silvestri. Who he left in Italy. He comes here and gets married again *here* –"

"So he's a – ? How is this a crisis someone has to do something without mercy, to so-called Maria Silvestri?"

"Giulio had a son."

"Richie's father. We know this."

"He had a previous son over there. Another Giulio who never came over. The father of so-called Maria Silvestri."

"She's related to Richie. Same grandfather, different grandmothers. And?"

"She claims Richie gave her the once over when she met him here. Undressed her visually. She tells Connie that she and Richie will have an affair and Richie will become a chip off Old Giulio's block. Become another Giulio with two women – doing the job to both. She's here to destroy Richie's marriage to get –"

"What, Rose?"

"Revenge for Giulio's first wife. Revenge for her grandmother. They will commit the revenge of incest."

"She's twisted, but Richie's not twisted. Just wants to give it to her once as hard as possible."

"Incest, Rock."

"Pretty mild incest, Rose."

"Mild, but still incest."

"And pretty hot for both because they know the incest factor when they're at it. I see their bodies –"

"Stop it, Rocky!"

"They can't wait to get in the sack. They do it right on the floor. Twice right on the floor."

"*Basta!* We can't let this happen to Richie's marriage."

"A week after his honeymoon, Ro, and this is what she and Richie want."

"What Silvestri wants. Who knows what Richie wants? Maybe not even Richie knows what Richie wants."

"Richie has no say, Rose. Richie wants only what his you-know-what wants."

"Put your post-game on. I'm calling my other godson. For advice. For a plan."

*

He turns on the TV for post-game analysis. Too late. Switches off and picks up *Ring Magazine*, the current issue, a remembrance of his late father's love – of Big Rocky himself who had so little time for him, but who'd brought home the monthly *Ring* for Little Rocky every month, starting with Little Rocky's ninth birthday. Until Big Rocky died. And Little Rocky had kept them all – piles of them, the yellowing presence of his father's care stacked in neat rows in the attic.

A sudden invasion of his sweet, painful memory by Rose's sharp, loud rebuke – a sound he's never heard when she talked to Godson Furillo: "You shock me beyond words, Joey! You should be ashamed of yourself! The day you're ashamed of yourself? That's the day when Jesus H returns to this broken earth in a jet-propelled gondola. You're not done hearing from me, Joey, believe you me." She slams down the receiver and walks back to her husband.

*

Rocky: I don't wanna say what I'm gonna say.

Rose: Don't say it. I already know.

Rocky: Until you hear it out loud from me, you don't know. You spoiled him from day one and he turned into a selfish shit. You asked him to help you out for Richie? He gave you nothing.

Rose: He says civilians are off the table. He doesn't involve himself with civilians. He says, We have our principles, just like the Church. He says to me, Russell wanted to do something to the Italian like you're implicating and I told Russell, Do that, Russell, and you go into the Mohawk River with your intestines on public display.

Rocky: You reminded him he involved himself on Richie's behalf for the Café? Someone high up in his Church – you, Rose, told him to help out your good grandson. You told him Richie needed a start in life and Russell encourages the building owner to give Richie a big break on rent or your brains are everywhere except inside your skull.

Rose: Out of respect for me he did that for Richie, and Richie got the space for the Café for a song and no requirement that he pay a portion of the annual taxes. He did that for me, yes, who when he was young I took over for his real mother, a g-d drunk who didn't do a thing for Joey. Joey did me a favor by doing a favor for Richie. Which Richie knows Joey stepped up for him, but he doesn't know I put the pressure on Joey.

Rocky: He did you a favor, but not out of respect for you. He respects no one. Shall I spell it out?

Rose: Don't.

Rocky: You know the truth.

Rose: Something has to be done to stop this Italian from destroying Richie's marriage. Sooner or later. Without mercy.

Rocky: What you have in mind? No decent person will do that.

*

The slightly built Professor, at 5'8", invites The Falcon for dinner and an evening of poetry – the muscular, light-complected, 6'3" Falcon, whose parents had come over from Sicily. (Who has ever seen a light-complected, 6'3" second generation Sicilian, whose parents were swarthy at 5'6" (mama) and 5'5" (papa)?) A dinner of Lebanese specialties, which the Professor's mother had taught him and which could not be found duplicated in any Lebanese deli, anywhere. Traditional recipes, but with unique variations – carried by Mintaha from her fog-enshrouded, remote mountain village in Lebanon.

In the last week of her life, The Professor promised his mother that he would divulge her secrets to no one. "Not even," she replied, "on the pain of death?" With her trade-mark mischievous grin, she added, in Arabic, "not even upon the demand of *Al Shaitan*, the Prince of Darkness?"

He knocks gently, The Prince of Darkness does, on The Professor's door, bearing a box of twelve cannoli from Café Romano – delivered by Richie's sexy cashier whose appearance provokes a painful fantasy, which all The Falcon's massive power cannot bring to realization. He does not bring the customary bottle of wine. He does not drink and will not indulge his host, if he, The Professor, does drink. And no wine at his table, ever, when he cooks for his out-of-town associates cuisine that yearns for the accompaniment of a forceful Red.

The Falcon has eaten two cannoli per day, seven days per week, for too many years. Such cannoli-practice has caused him, in his words, to "have trouble with his clustered hole." He was taking a heavy dose of Lipitor, but it did no good. His doctor advised that he needed to cut the cannolis "completely, Mr. Furillo, or at least reduce your addiction to seven, rather than fourteen per week." The Falcon said, "How would you like to cut your addiction to breathing?"

Who in Upstate New York doesn't know the frightening biggest thing about The Falcon? The Professor is convinced of another big thing – less big, but big enough. About this other thing, the rumor is widespread, but only The Professor believes that The Falcon is a gourmet cook of Italian fare and that except for her syrup-drowned pancakes, Mrs. Falcon never cooks. Without love, the Don prepares lunches and dinners for his wife. With strategic love, he cooks for the boys from Buffalo, who never smile when they come to Utica to discuss irreversible contracts.

The Mafia Chief and The Distinguished Professor of Poetry. The man of violence, who touches the world and causes actual change – call it population control – versus the man of the mind, who dreams that literary ideas, his especially, will create social change, though these ideas, especially his, never do. The literary man works hard not to think of the "i-word," but fails to keep it from invading his daylight hours. Impotent. Impotent. Impotent.

The besuited Professor opens the door to his guest, who is also besuited because to step out into public without creating a *bella figura* would bring shame upon himself – a fate worse, he knows, than a bullet in the brain. Unlike The Falcon, The Professor is not driven by Italian custom, but is nevertheless besuited in and outside the house, from morning to bedtime – as if he had something to conceal. What he needs to conceal he works hard not to know.

An awkward two seconds of silence that feels for both like two hours. They're dressed in identical pinstriped, double-breasted suits from Armani. The Falcon's acquired for no cost, The Professor's acquired at full cost: $4,095.

The Professor says, "Welcome, sir. Good evening. Welcome."

The Falcon says, "This is for you." (Handing him the box of cannoli.)

The Professor says, "Thank you, sir. Nice suit, Don Joseph. Almost as nice as mine."

The Falcon says, "With your comedy, Prof, your balls are bigger than I thought."

The Professor says, "Thank you on behalf of my hefty gonads" – and motions him inside, where he has inserted an extra leaf into his lustrous African-Rosewood dining table, now eight feet long and accommodating the nine Lebanese specialties he has set there. Place settings at either end.

The Professor, opening the box of cannoli, says, "Twelve cannoli! Such an expense, sir!"

The Falcon says, "Know what those are, Prof?"

The Professor says, "A trick question, sir?"

The Falcon says, "Poems you eat." (He gestures to the Lebanese specialties. He's never seen these before.) "From out of your Syrian background, Prof?"

"Lebanese, sir. 100% Lebanese."

"That's what those Syrians always say." (Then, in a high-pitched whine:) "Me no Syrian! Me Lebanese! I once knew a Syrian who claimed he was Lebanese. His wife was white bread from out of town. She was beautiful."

"'Was,' Don Joseph?"

"She went. He's still here, the so-called Lebanese."

"She died?"

"You have to use that word?"

"You knew her?"

"Russell did. As they say on that TV show, Up Close and Personal."

"She had an affair with Mr. Martello?"

"Never thought of it like that."

The Professor catches the drift and changes the subject as he begins to circle the table, pointing to each dish: "Kibbeh. Knafeh jibneh. Hummus. Rice Pilaf. Manakish. Tabbouleh. Sfeeha. Pita Bread. Fattoush."

The Falcon says, "I have to know the names to eat them?"

The Professor says, "Shall I compare thee to a summer's day?"

The Falcon pauses. He stares dangerously. He speaks softly, almost in a whisper: "I realize not all you single guys are one of those. You one of those? No skin off my back. Live and let live. More or less."

The Professor says, "Thou art more lovely and temperate."

"Prof, you're walking a thin line."

"I am quoting poetry, Don Joseph – not making a you-know-what move on you. Poultry, Don Joseph, from The Bard of Avon. Shakespeare, sir."

"Avon? I heard in high school that Shakespeare was from England. Am I wrong? He was a Limey, right?"

"He was."

"You're a professor? Avon's a little village outside of Rochester. You don't know this? And you're a professor? A serious friend of mine lives there."

"I presume, Don Joseph, that our Avon was named after the English Avon, where Shakespeare was born."

"I'll tell my friend in Avon that you presume. Or maybe I won't. He's the type he flies off the handle at the drop of a presumption."

"You're a funny man."

"What?"

"I mean thou art witty."

"Really? You think so? Thee and thou. Yeah. Nice. Too bad those words are out of circulation. Too bad, if you ask me. Because 'you' is an ugly sound. Fuck you. You are fucked. If Martello would say Fuck thee. Thou art fucked – if Russell would only say it that way at the end of his intimate affairs, people might not mind the end, if they're hearing Shakespeare sounds, which are tender in my opinion. Something tender at the end of the affair instead of – can we dig into this beautiful stuff? How about we start with that one?"

"Knafeh, Don Joseph. More or less a dessert. I suggest we eat it with a cannoli or two at the end, if you don't mind, sir."

"You 'suggest'? Who made this rule? You? I don't care for this so-called rule. Take the cannoli. Morning, noon, and night, I take the cannoli. Because this rule doesn't decide. I decide. Or you 'suggesting' it's your house, you decide?"

"My house, Don Joseph, is your house."

"What's it made out of, Prof?"

"It's a kind of cheese cake."

"Cheese cake? I have an associate in Miami, we're very close. He sends me two cheese cakes, gigantic. Every Christmas. This broadminded Jew honors my Catholicism with a Jew cake for Christmas. You Catholic?"

"In a way. Knafeh, sir, combines mozzarella and ricotta, sugar and butter, crushed pistachios mixed in, all wrapped in phyllo dough and covered in a warm bath of orange blossom syrup."

The Falcon cuts a chunk of knafeh and adds two cannoli to begin the meal as The Professor reads and "explicates," as he puts it, in slow detail, word by word, including "and" and "the," the entirety of Sonnet #18. The Professor does not eat. He talks, savoring the pleasurable image of the torture and death of the tormenter of his youth, the wheel-chair confined Michael Caco.

The Falcon listens to the interpretation of Sonnet #18, but is not responding as he samples dish after dish – now the kibbeh and fattoush, chewing and gazing he is at the art on the dining room wall: the charcoal rendering of two robust figures, male and female, nude and thick-thighed in an embrace. And there's another, a charcoal rendering of a male figure, not robust – slight, fragile, sitting in a chair and almost disappearing under the embrace of a huge, thick-bodied female – she's nude, she's sitting in his lap – he's happy to disappear beneath and inside her thick-bodied embrace. On the wall opposite, a painting in grey tones of a man and a woman in ordinary clothes, their heads and faces helmeted – armored faces but without openings for eyes. The Falcon is thinking of the walls of his own dining room, covered with his wife's family photos of smiling adults and children. No photos on his dining room wall of his father, who left when The Falcon was two, or of his mother who left, absented in alcohol, or of the older woman, the Godmother – no photo of her, Rose DiCastro, who loved him as no one ever had.

He's caught enough of The Professor's explication of Shakespeare
– The Professor had said "explication" which he, The Falcon, figured a
high-ass substitute for "explanation." Why wasn't "explanation" good
enough? Fancy words they hold over us lower asses. The Falcon says,
"There's a song by Peggy Lee, *Is That All There Is?* You're telling me
Shakespeare is informing me things change? We get old? We lose our
looks? Including the good-looking people? Except for her? She has
eternal summer? She doesn't die? Because of this poem she gets so-
called immortality?"

The Professor says, "Exactly."

"But, Prof, he gives no picture of her in the poem."

"There's a reason for that, Don Joseph."

"Okay," The Falcon says, "I give myself one guess. If he described
this babe she'd look real, like any woman. She wouldn't look like eternal
summer or immortal because those things you can't put in a picture,
where you draw a real face that can't match up to something never seen
by nobody, in this world full of faces you wish you never saw."

The Professor says, "You deserve an A+ if you were my student."

"Trying to get on my good side?"

"Don Joseph, all of your sides are good."

"You're wily. *That*, they didn't teach you in college. To talk like *that*."

"Only speaking the truth, Don Joseph."

"You know what the truth is, Prof? Advanced bullshit."

"Much truth in what you say, sir, according to advanced literary theory."

"Your Shakespeare is over-the-top arrogant. He thinks his poem
gives her eternal life? How many people in the history of this world of
morons have read that poem – compared to the one my high school
teacher read a hundred times to us, where I was half-asleep at my desk,
with my head down on the desk? His love, this guy moans, is like a red,
red rose. Know that one, Prof?"

"I do."

"So I'm half-asleep one time and I hear those words and I sit up
straight and from my sleep I say, 'But what about those things roses
have? Mrs. Reamer, what about the fucking thorns?' The funny thing,
Prof, she reacts with a smile, she says to me, 'Mr. Joey Furillo, you
have a brilliant future ahead of you as a close reader of people. The

close reading you do may very well save your life, Mr. Furillo.' What happens after that, Prof? This goody two shoes in the class goes to the principal. I got suspended for a week for using the F-word and she got fired on the spot. That goody two shoes? I gave him something special and they call him after that to this day, David one ear. The principal on a monthly basis gets four slashed tires. He accidentally damages his knee caps beyond repair. Mush."

The Professor says, "I am speechless."

The Falcon says, "You just spoke."

The Professor says, "I wish to tell you something about Joni that you may not know. At the peak of her career, hit after hit, she was dominating the charts, as they say. She quits singing at 32. To take care of her gravely-ill husband. At 32, Don Joseph."

The Falcon says, "I knew that."

The Professor says, "What a woman!"

The Falcon says, "A woman like that doesn't exist anymore. You know why? Because we live in a world of perverts."

They rise and go to the door, where they embrace. The Professor's head nestled against The Falcon's chest.

*

The Woman From Naples – Maria Romano, who calls herself Maria Silvestri – chose to live at Hotel Utica because its name suggested her strongest fantasy: A hotel in the grand Italian mode, with an immense echoing lobby and rooms – even those not suites – twice the size of the average hotel room – featuring, everywhere, including in the bathrooms, fixtures of marble, gold, and silver – and dining rooms staffed by waiters in tuxedos, accompanied by waiters-in-training, also in tuxedos and bearing menus spilling over five gilt-edged pages.

Upon arrival at Hotel Utica she found a lobby of frayed carpeting, walls of fading dark brown paint fast becoming walls of baby-shit brown and a receptionist, clad in what she'd worn for three days in succession, who had apparently showered only an hour before in cheap cologne. The Italian Stranger is undeterred. She requests the celebrated Presidential Suite on the 13th floor.

The Receptionist says, "Credit card."

The Italian says, "I do not have that thing. I have American money."

The Receptionist, adjusting her bra, says, "I'm not supposed to take real money because of a Spic counterfeit ring up here in central New York, but in your case as a more or less white European – you're mainly white, correct? How many nights you planning?"

The Italian Stranger says, "Who can know such things for certain?"

The Receptionist says, "What things? What things you referring?"

The Italian says, "How many days you need?"

The Receptionist says, "Seven. Seven times 200. Up front. 1400 clams."

The Italian peels off 14 one hundred dollar bills. The Receptionist sweeps the crisp new bills across the counter to her side and below, out of sight. 700 for the Hotel. 700 for herself.

Overcome with the great, good feeling of sudden prosperity, the Receptionist tells the Italian, "Famous people slept in the Presidential Suite. President Franklin Delano Roosevelt. Can you swallow that?"

The Italian knew that Roosevelt was famous for doing good things, but did not know what those good things were.

The Receptionist says, "For your information, Mae West slept there too, but not at the same time as Roosevelt the cripple."

The Italian knew the wonderful words: A hard man is good to find. Are ya' happy to see me, Big Boy, or is that a banana in your pocket?

She says to the Receptionist, "Mae West is more famous in my country than your President Frank."

The Receptionist says, "Hoppy slept there too."

"Who is Happy?"

"Hoppy! Not happy. Hopalong Cassidy, famous movie cowboy."

The Italian hears "Cassidy" as a mangled pronunciation of an Italian idiom: *Che si dice?* (Hey! What's up?) and responds, "I do not discuss my privacy."

The Receptionist, shrugging, says, handing her the key, "Take the elevator over there." Adjusts her bra.

The Italian says, "Write down the names who slept in my bed. I will forget in my bed, in the dark."

The Receptionist says, "They're on a plaque on your door, which will be replaced soon to add a fourth name. You know Judy Garland

and Mickey Mantle? They slept in your bed. As far as I know, not at the same time. The owners decided one of those two will make it onto the new plaque."

"Which one?" says The Italian. "I hope Judy."

The Receptionist says, "Judy the fag lover didn't make the team. Mickey was a real man."

In the Presidential Suite she finds, here and there, peeling wall paper, hardwood floors no longer gleaming, two king-sized beds, one small bathroom with a stained bidet, a bowl of fruit, long past its prime, and a pamphlet entitled *The Sights of Utica, How to Get There From Here*. She sits with the pamphlet and broods to the verge of tears, as she imagines the Utica Zoo. How to free the emaciated animals from their foul cages. How to lure the Director of the Zoo to his death, fed fully conscious to a starving adult Malayan tiger. As a child she had been taken to a private zoo of lame animals on the outskirts of Rome. It was adjacent to that other abomination, *Cinema Città*, where famous Italian films were made and their toxins vomited out to the world and all who prefer the cancer of illusion.

She will not visit the Utica zoo. Or the numerous pizzerias which dominate the sights of Utica, sixteen of them, located in every section of town, including the run-down Polish West Side and its popular Polack Pizzeria (the actual name: look it up) specializing in pierogi-studded pies. Or the six bakeries along a 200 yard stretch of Bleecker, the main artery of the Italian-American East Side. Utica College? Who needs it? The Historical Society? No. Or Zeinas Lebanese Café, or Pho Mekong House of Noodles, or Ventura's Restaurant, where Joe DiMaggio once ate, or Henrietta's Hawaiian Islands Bar and Grill. Or: We Design Your Funeral Flowers Sooner or Later. She resisted, barely, the temptation of the abandoned Utica State Asylum for the Insane. Abandoned because all of Utica was now in its right mind – or else everywhere, in all sections, forever mad.

The Italian Stranger had come to town to lash out with her long-festering lunacy. She will not resist Café Romano. She is eager for the vast and lush greenery of Proctor Park, where she will meet a man with assassination in his heart, whose name is Rocco DiCastro.

*

Seven years have passed since they'd graduated from Proctor High – seven years since they'd seen each other, when they cross paths at the Chicago Market and Russell Martello is immediately flooded by a rush of desire for what he has not, and believes he'll never have: the body of Connie O'Donnell. And she, since just the day before, had imagined, still imagines, her husband's secret passion for Maria Silvestri, and had heard, still hears, the Italian Woman's barely disguised intention to bed Richie, whose appetite for Connie was white hot. (It was, wasn't it?) It seemed obvious – was she deluded? – that he, a little more than a week since their honeymoon, was seized by the desire to transgress. Actual physical consummation, she thought, was a trivial consequence of the explosive consummation that had already transpired, in his mind.

Martello stands at the wall of produce, facing the section of Bell Peppers. At a discreet distance, and from behind, Connie sees him. In his shopping cart: a single unripe banana, slightly curved, hard: six inches. And a carrot, thick, palm-filling, with little tapering toward its end: six inches. And a cucumber of not unreasonable girth or length. Nothing else in the cart.

She moves to her left to gather a three-quarters view. He's lost the soft fleshy look of his high school days. Narrow-waisted now, so much the better to emphasize his broad shoulders. V-shaped Russell. Short-sleeved shirt, strong forearms and biceps. (Must work out.) A Clark Gable mustache. Aviator sunglasses. Russell Martello has become darkly charismatic. She could turn and move quickly to the far side of the market, disappear amid the aisles of alcohol and cleaning fluids, and avoid the awkwardness of an encounter after all these years, but before she can act on the impulse to hide he turns and sees her, two peppers in one of his large hands, one yellow, the other orange. In the other hand, a big red one. (Is he good, very good, with his hands?)

The look on his face: Is he happy to see her or is he in a coma? What Martello sees upon first seeing Connie: Kindness, she is the soul of kindness, as always. Kindness, he imagines, at the verge of gratifying his long yearning – the two of them gliding through the gap that has separated their bodies, to be embraced tightly by Connie O'Donnell.

The Falcon's much-experienced hit man speaks:

"My God! For heaven's sake! And mine too!" He blushes. "My God, Connie!" He raises his arms, with peppers-laden hands.

She takes a step toward him: "Russell! It's been much too long. How very good to see you."

They move toward one another, embrace, bodies properly angled, groins almost free of contact, Russell's hands still laden.

"So good, Connie."

"Where is it, Russell? I don't see it. Are you hiding it?"

"Where is what, Connie? What am I hiding? Tell me."

"Your sausage. I don't see the succulent sausage."

(He does not faint.)

Has Connie O'Donnell become someone else? Known always for her chaste ways, who is she now at the Chicago Market? Through their high school years she was keenly aware of Martello's unrequited and unrequitable crush. She believes that he will bear the agony until welcomed by the grave's tight embrace. But now, at the wall of produce? Connie the Cock Teaser?

What had flowed through her mind so suddenly to transform her? In a fragment of a second at the speed of light: *Betray Richie with a killer before Richie you bastard betrays me.* So rapidly through consciousness with little awareness – or deep below consciousness without awareness, with strong propulsive feeling emerging in erotically charged language which drives Russell to the edge of spontaneous orgasm or heart failure, a hard attack, then and there before the wall of produce.

"Sausage and peppers on the menu tonight?"

"Not for me, Connie. For Mr. Furillo. He's got the sausage. He's always got the sausage, but he ran out of peppers, why I'm here. He runs out of peppers, lucky me, I get to see you again, thank God."

"He's cooking for you?"

"I wish."

"You could learn. Not hard."

"Spicy hot, Connie, or sweet and mild?"

"I like it hot, Russell. You?"

"Either way."

"Some can't take it hot."

"I can, Connie."

"Me too, Russell. I take it easily."

"Christ Jesus!"

"Jesus doesn't take it at all. As far as we know."

"You really think I could learn to cook sausage and peppers?"

"Richie claims he has business in Albany and won't be home until around midnight. Come over for dinner, why don't you? I'll make sausage and peppers for you and teach you step by step the way I was taught. By someone who calls herself The Girl Who Eats Everything. Come at 6. Wouldn't you like to come?"

"Dream on," he says. Though he has been dreaming of her forever.

3.

On The Occasion Of A Corpse

SEVEN GATHER ON this late afternoon of fading September light: Don Joseph (The Falcon) Furillo, Rosario (Russell) Martello, Rocco and Rose DiCastro, Connie O'Donnell and Richie Romano, and The Professor. Or are they nine? Giulio Romano is there, so to speak, and she, too, the Italian Stranger, in her distracting absence. All gathered on the first floor of The Falcon's house on upper Taylor Ave. All ignoring what lies, in stillness, in Don Joseph's front living room – what lies inside the nauseating odor of too many flowers at peak of bloom in a room needing the relief of outdoor air: No windows thrown open because this is Utica, city of violent swings of weather, which trigger dreams of Florida and "getting the hell out of this town for good."

In a period of several weeks: from the heavy humidity of late summer and 95 degrees, to the dry heat of early fall and the low 70s, now today at 48 degrees with a slicing wind out of the northwest, and the incredible forecast of rain and sleet changing to snow flurries around midnight. The heat in the house is on to accompany the bitter, cascading condemnations of Utica and its entire history, as they savor, slowly, Italian specialties prepared especially for the event of the front room.

*

The Falcon in the kitchen will not curse. Nor will he raise his voice, not even a little, when the fine dinner plate slips from his hand, crashes to the floor, and breaks into two clean pieces. No shards, no virtually invisible particles that refuse to reveal themselves until he shuffles the next morning to the kitchen, groggy with sleep, and steps barefoot into reality. The surprise of physical pain will not diminish the new found pain of his happiness.

Don Furillo is not alone in the kitchen when – with a will of its own – the plate slips away. Another voice, that of hit man Russell Martello shouts, "Oh, Lordy! Oh, Don Furillo!"

The Professor in the dining room says, cheerfully, "This is the truth, ladies and gentlemen: If a cr-cr-cr-cracked dish is boiled for 45 minutes in sweet milk, the crack will be so welded together that it will be almost invisible, and so strong that it will stand the same usage as before."

From the kitchen The Falcon says, "What I love about The Prof. What I love."

Rocky D says, "What's sweet milk? Chocolate milk for kids?"

Rosie D says, "He means regular full fat milk. Normal milk, Rock. Not that low or no fat crap like drinking chalk."

Rocky says, "So why does he say sweet milk? Because professors have to talk the way normal people don't?"

The Professor says, "To whiten laces, wash them in sour milk. That too is the truth."

Rocky says, "Who keeps sour milk?"

Richie says, "Does he mean make dirty white laces white again? Or turn black or brown laces white? Does anyone smell racism here?"

Connie says, "He's teaching. He's just a teacher. Relax, Prof, and become one of us forever."

The Prof says, "Wait! Wax your ashtrays and the ashes won't cling."

Rocky says, "No wonder he moans about being lonely."

The Prof says, "Wait! Ma-Ma-Marigolds prevent rodents."

Connie says, "Let's show a little mercy. Give The Professor the plate of prosciutto and those figs big like pears."

From the kitchen, between giggles, The Falcon says, "Save me some of that prosciutto and figs or I'll make you pay with your life."

Russell, leaving the kitchen, hugging four large bottles of San Pellegrino, says, "Let's show some respect for the old guy out there by himself in the flowers. Only the Lord knows what's on his mind."

Rosie D says, "Happiness is like potato salad." (Forks and spoons freeze mid-air.)

Rosie D says, "Tell us, Professor, what was it like over there? In Oxford. Did you write your thesis on potato salad?"

Richie says, "Godmother, why do you tease The Professor? Why do I have the urge to join you?"

Connie says, "Big Rich, down deep you have no respect for these intellectual types. Who does? On the surface we're civil, but –"

From the kitchen, The Falcon, this time richly in song:

LIFE IS JUST A BOWL OF CHERRIES –
DON'T TAKE IT SERIOUS –
LIFE IS TOO MYSTERIOUS –
YOU WORK, YOU SAVE, YOU WORRY SO –
BUT YOU CAN'T TAKE YOUR DOUGH –
WHEN YOU GO GO GO …

He pauses. Then again, softly:

WHEN YOU GO GO GO –

Rocky says, "Russell, what's he making in the kitchen? We heard about his culinary greatness. What's he making in there?"

Russell says, "He told me not to say. He's got a heck of a voice, don't you think?"

Richie says, "Sinatra with balls. Sinatra without the constant pissing and moaning about the one who got away. Snotra."

Russell says, "Oh, Rich! He'd love that!"

Rosie says, "Respect? When are we going to show it to the man – the man in the front room? Can we even call him a man? It's a male, but let's be honest. It's not a man."

Connie says, "Where's The Falcon's wife? What's her name? Why isn't she here?"

The Prof says, "Her name's – he calls her The Mall Fucker."

Rocky says, "The Mall Fucker lives upstairs."

Connie says, "He doesn't invite The Mall Fucker to this grievous occasion. Why? Because she's wide open for someone at the Mall?"

From the kitchen:

ALONE FROM NIGHT TO NIGHT SHE HAUNTS ME –
TOO WEAK TO BREAK THE CHAINS THAT BIND ME –
I NEED NO SHACKLES TO REMIND ME –
I'M JUST A PRISONER OF LOVE!

The Professor says, "This is the final truth: We're all broken-hearted. Alone. We're all in agony most of the time."

The Falcon again:

I NEED NO SHACKLES TO REMIND ME –

Rocky says, "I'll tell you this, kids. The wife upstairs? He's not her prisoner. I'll tell you that."

The Professor, "He's shackled. He's in the pain of desire. The pain is a warm ba-ba-bath."

Rocky, "Prof, tell the true truth. The warm bath of pain. You love it too. It arouses you. It gives you a –"

From the kitchen:

THOUGH SHE HAS ANOTHER –
I CAN'T HAVE ANOTHER –
FOR I'M NOT FREE!

Connie: "Rich, he's really beginning to scare me."
Richie: "Welcome to the club."

SHE'S IN MY DREAMS –
AWAKE OR SLEEPING –
UPON MY KNEES TO HER I'M CREEPING –

Russell: "Now you all know how I feel."

WHAT'S THE GOOD OF MY CARING –
IF SOMEONE IS SHARING –
THOSE ARMS WITH ME?

The Prof: "The Falcon is losing it. Is his competitor in this room? Who is the "she" who haunts him, awake or sleeping?"

*

At Utica's proper funeral homes, the three-day ritual of mourning ends at mid-day on the third day, but the dead, despite being the subject of the Wake, do not awake and arise again when the funeral cortège begins and the cars carrying the bereaved family, the friends of the family, and the friends of the friends of the family line up, with the corpse-bearing hearse at the head of the line. They travel at a crawl to the cemetery, where early that morning the grave is freshly excavated, where the shovelers will stand apart from the mourners, smoking and waiting under a clump of trees, while the mourners each place a single rose on the closed coffin lid, then leave to return to their pre-three day lives and not witness the shovelers flick away their unfiltered cigarettes and lumber from their lurking place under the clump of trees to lower the coffin into the grave. Always, one mourner will stand shoulder to shoulder with the shovelers and refuse to leave until he hears the clods hit, with a deep thud, the coffin lid below.

But there yet remains in East Utica the stubborn contingent of those who will not relinquish the old way of the Wake – to be conducted not at a funeral home proper but at the house of the deceased, now Richie's house, no longer Giulio's. The pleasure and honor of hosting unhoused Giulio's Wake is all mine, The Falcon insisted, without opposition. At The Falcon's house the old way prevails with food overflowing and conversation ranging without deference, serenely detached from the solemn occasion and the memory of the one in The Falcon's front room – where Giulio's mourners have yet to pay their formal respects by kneeling and praying before his coffin.

*

Massive platters, more massive than massive, of six Italian delights, each of which bear enough for 14 hungry of body and spirit (though they are but seven). Under catastrophic structural pressure, the table creaks and grinds. And beneath the creaking and grinding, a dark groaning of *basso profondo*.

Courtesy of The Godmother: classic prosciutto and figs and her legendary calzones. From The Professor – who else? connoisseur of complexity – a salad of finocchio, celery, artichoke hearts, black olives (pitted), hard-boiled eggs, salami (too much, which is never too much), scallions, lemon juice, olive oil (more, of course, than the recipe calls for), but no capers because capers rip him apart, and wine vinegar. From hit man Martello: Stuffed mushrooms (bread crumbs, chopped onion, grated cheese (pecorino only), parsley and basil basil basil prepared with ferocity by enforcer Russell, who would like to stuff anybody's mushroom, all thirteen genders welcome. From Rocky D: Sausage and peppers in the oven: 8 sweet and 8 hot Italian sausages, 10 frying peppers (yellow and orange) – for this is the last pleasure of Rocky D who says, as he places his platter heavily, I didn't forget the onions and the garlic, and I'm trying to forget my former hot Italian sausage and pray that my wife doesn't ever forget. From Connie: Spaghetti Carbonara, Connie style, who says, if you're Italian you don't need me, an Irish lass, in your midst, to tell you I make it better than you've ever had it in your eager wet mouths. And meatballs, almost the size of cantaloupes, and two dozen cannoli from the artist of pastry, Richie Romano.

And the chewing and the chomping and the smacking of the lips. And The Falcon's mystery contribution, yet to come.

*

She, Rose DiCastro, says, "*Che vergogna!*"

Richie says, "Amen to that! Translate for us dummies, Godmother."

Rose says, "*Vergogna!* It is truly a *vergogna* that I have to translate for you supposed Italians."

Connie says, "I'm married to one, I'm not one, but I need no translation. *Vergogna* you should know is shame. You should be ashamed of yourselves because we haven't paid our respects to Giulio Romano. We talk like comedians and eat like bears, big as tanks, getting ready to go into hibernation, but we haven't gone to the front room."

Rose DiCastro rises. With the exception of her husband Rocky, they all move to what lies in the front room, where all the shades are drawn.

Rocky goes to The Falcon's study and turns on the TV.

At the coffin they kneel, one by one, on the thing called the kneeler, to pay formal respect and to pray – beginning with The Professor, who speaks softly but clearly to all except Russell whose hearing is failing in his late 20s, thanks to too many hours of unprotected practice at the gun range. The Professor says, slowly, a Hail Mary, then more slowly yet, the Lord's Prayer, better known among Catholics as the Our Father, Who Art in Heaven, hallowed be Thy Name. And extremely slowly, in a chant, the Act of Contrition – "Oh! My God, I am heartily sorry for having offended Thee, and because I offend THEE my God, I dread the loss of Heaven and the pains of Hell." Russell hears not "heartily sorry," but "hardly sorry," and he begins to heat up. Then Richie and Connie pray call and response, "Lord have mercy, Christ have mercy," which Martello hears as "Lord have misery, Christ have misery" and quickly reaches the boiling point and begins to sway and mumble, "Blessed are the poor, for they shall inherit shit." Rose puts her hand on his shoulder, strokes the back of his head and whispers, "The Lord is with you in this your hour of rage." Then she kneels, Rosary in hand, and says, "God welcomes you, Giulio, to the comfort of His eternity." Then Russell, feeling a little peace, kneels, stares at Giulio's face, touches Giulio's cold hand for 30 seconds, then rises, wiping away a furtive tear.

They retreat to the groaning table, except for Rose, who finds Rocky watching the Yankees take on the Orioles of Baltimore. With his eyes glued to the screen, Rocky says, "How they lose to this lousy team, year in and year out, drives me nuts. It's killing me."

She says, "Turn that thing off now and get over to the front room or else – how many years we've been married, Rock?"

He says, "49, which you know, why ask me?"

"Turn that thing off, get in their right now and pay your respects right now or you'll never see the 50th. What you're doing here is a complete disgrace."

"You're getting extreme, Ro," he says, and turns off the game and goes to the kneeler, but he does not kneel.

She says, "Kneel. And this better be sincere, or we're finished. Kneel."

He says, "You talking divorce at our age? If you don't like how I sound when I pray?"

She says, "Let's hear your prayer. I'll let you know after I hear how you talk to the Lord. Kneel."

He kneels.

*

All at table, but now without appetite and in silence.

From the kitchen:

IT HAD TO BE YOU –
IT HAD TO BE YOU –
I WANDERED AROUND –
AND FINALLY FOUND –
THE SOMEBODY WHO –
COULD MAKE ME BE TRUE –
COULD MAKE ME BE BLUE –

The Falcon enters at last, saying, "This. This is it. The real Sicilian thing. Here it is."

The Professor says, "Don Joseph, it had to be you. You are the real Sicilian thing. What's that beautiful thing that you bring to us? Does it have a name?"

The Falcon says, "Everything has a name. *Sfincione di San Vito.* Invented by nuns near Palermo, who were Sicilians first and nuns second. Prof, you're a big deal scholar. Do your homework then tell my sad guests here what you find about what I bring from the basement of my Sicilian heart."

Richie says, "Who killed Giulio Romano? Who killed my grandfather, Don Joseph?"

Connie says, "Where is the mysterious Italian, Don Joseph? Who's not here. Where is she with or against her will?"

Gesturing with quick jabs toward Richie and Connie, as if shoving in the point of a knife, the Don says, "What have I done – what have I done to deserve insults? Especially from you two? Anyone else have questions? No? None? You sure? Good. Now eat. Eat like there's no fuckin' tomorrow."

4.

The Professor To Himself

I SIT ON my front porch in humid summer twilight, watching Big Anthony waddle by in a dark suit and long red tie, down to and covering his crotch. I would like to stop him. I would like to say, Big Anthony, Why do you call yourself an undertaker? When you, as undertaker, actually undertake, what exactly do you undertake in the forbidden back area of your funeral home? Do you wash your hands and enjoy coffee and pastries on your break, after you drain the blood, inject the embalming fluid, with delicate finger tips smear make up on the face and hands of the corpse, stuff cotton in the nose and anus of the dearly departed, to prevent leakage, and do what you do to the erect penis of the dead but still horny male – what exactly do you do to – or shall I say "with" – the rigorous penis in order to grant its last explosive pleasure? You dress the corpse in his best suit – after which, and only then, do you generously apply after-shave, or perfume as the case may be. Big Anthony, I would like to say, when you practice life's only necessary art, making them ... almost good-looking, you undertake by taking them under. Or, you burn them at 2,000 degree Fahrenheit, in order to release them into the air, so that we, the living, will inhale the dead and give them yet another unhappy life.

Why not, Big Anthony, why not call yourself a mortician? Like a musician, the mortician plays the corpsechord. I imagine Big Anthony answering, You sad sack – you consider yourself educated? Then he would waddle off, jiggling under his loose-fitting suit.

In their grief, the next of kin will not enter into struggle with Big Anthony to lower his fee, which is heftier than himself. In their grief, money does not enter and Big Anthony knows this. They write the check quickly and Big Anthony is happy.

When, in my imagination, I ask him why he chose his life work, he answers, I like to help people, Professor, just like you do. That's what I do. I help people. Unlike you, Mr. Ph.D., I don't think my shit doesn't stink. Then I would say, Ph.D.? Guess what it stands for? Tell me, Prof, he says, you're one of those. Big Anthony, I say, Ph.D. stands for Piled High and Deeper. I hear him say, I suddenly like you, Prof, and promise to treat you gently when the time comes, in the forbidden back room of my funeral home.

*

Big Anthony is known by his full name: Anthony Gigliotti. Or as AG the Undertaker. Or just as AG, the one and only, who is asked too many times, as if it's the greatest joke ever. "Hey! Big AG! How's business?" All joking ceases when AG finds the best retort: "Business is always good, Angelo, even in tough times, when I offer modest discounts on coffins, to demonstrate my humanity. And deeper discounts to those who wish, in their youth and glowing health, to secure a coffin in advance of the day of need. My dear, Angelo, you're young and vigorous like a stud bull. How does 50% off sound?"

*

They call me The Professor. Or Prof (as if we were buddies). Or Doc. They say, with a touch of mockery, "What's up, Doc?" Do they think of me as Professor Bugs Bunny, my Ph.D. granted at the College of Bedlam? Someone at Café Romano insists on calling me Bobby, though "Bobby," he knows, is not my name. (His name is "Bobby.") I envy Big A, whose name is spoken respectfully in his presence. (Of course, they fear him.) A week ago his name was spoken with concern when someone at the Café says, "I hear Anthony's daughter has been hit by leukemia." Someone else says, "I saw him. He looks scared." I, the Prof, have never been married. Have no daughter or son. May my unborn savor their good fortune.

Do they, the talkers and watchers at Café Romano, ever wonder what The Prof is like when he is sick? Do they imagine The Prof in love, or if he's ever been in love – and was denied reciprocity? Is it possible for him to be sad, but never show it? What causes The Prof to be afraid? What makes him tremble? He seems lost inside his head whenever we see him. What's inside his head? Or is he bored with our company at the Café? He rarely says a word. He sits at our table. He sips his cappuccino. He's here, but not here. Surely he sighs and suffers, but only in the privacy of his house. Unheard and unseen.

*

At no time of day, no day of the year does an undertaker walk by my front porch. In my vicinity there's a family named Gigliotti, but none work in the funeral racket, none are called Anthony, and all are short of stature and slight of build. I am a fantasist, a silent storyteller, and an occasional stutterer. A fantasist maybe because a stutterer. In my classrooms, especially in large lecture halls, I am fluent and smooth, like a classical singer producing with seeming ease a long line of connected notes, as if never breathing. I perform, I sing. I do not speak, not really, which is the reason I do not stutter in the lecture hall. In conversation I sometimes stammer. I become angry as I get glued to the first syllable or first letter of a word. Then I explode in a flood of non-stammering rage and sing sonofabitchin-motherfucker-goddamn-bastard-Jesus-shithead Christ.

Unfortunately I cannot be the fluent vehicle of rage in what is called polite company. At the Dean's annual dinner for distinguished faculty I stare and collapse inside myself and compose stories that do not reach the ears or eyes of others. Inside, in my silence, I become a little crowd of characters and get to say all the lines, the witty, the brutal, the beautiful. No more me. No more loneliness. The Prof is finally free.

How is it that I speak easily and at times wittily with The Falcon? I believe that we like each other. He is exceptionally intelligent and could have made a first rate literary critic. He comes to my house and leaves his hit man and body guard outside, idling in the Mercedes. I could have "whacked" him and become a significant paragraph in Mafia history. How easy it would have been. When I was describing the various Lebanese dishes to come around behind him, as he sat, and slash his throat, and the carotid artery would have gushed like a fire hose. Years ago I saw it, the fire hose of blood, in my summer work at the slaughterhouse. He would have had no chance.

Instead of slashing his throat, I gorged and talked about Shakespeare. He was brilliant. He implied strongly that he would like me to "do the job" on The Italian Stranger. He had heard me voice my desire to kill Michael Caco, which he found ridiculous. Their language of killing is delightfully vivid. Like poetry. Whack. Do the job – which is also used to say "fuck her," in the literal sense. Delightful. "Put her on a slab" is so much more satisfying than "eliminate" or even "terminate with extreme prejudice," as CIA types put it. The CIA euphemism is not vivid. It's a form of wit that appeals to those who think their shit doesn't stink.

The word on the street is The Falcon has been hit with an overmastering passion for The Italian. I was thinking of telling The Falcon a story about my summer job at the Thom McAn shoe store, when I was 16. One afternoon, in she comes, exceptionally attractive in her mid-twenties. She looked around at some leotards, didn't buy, and left. The assistant manager, Vic Broccoli (really), knew her name. He tells me and the manager, Larry, who looked like an Italian Rock Hudson, what he'd like to do with the young woman. He says, "I want to sell her a hand-fitted leotard." Her name was Mirella and she was a recent Italian immigrant. You see where this is going? I was going to tell The Falcon that it was I, not Vic Broccoli, who spoke the desire to sell her a hand-fitted leotard. In view of the development of his romantic feelings for The Italian Stranger, he might have concluded that I was his competitor for Maria Silvestri. And put me on a slab.

5.

They Gather In His Name

IN THE LATE afternoon, Richie Romano, Connie O'Donnell, Rose and Rocky DiCastro, and The Professor – and even hit man Russell Martello – each receive, by courier, this note:

> Café Romano 9 pm sharp one week from today sharp. Be there. Do not inform anyone of your reseat of this message or the message what it says. Nobody. Inclusive of a person you may or may not be in conjugal relations should you achieve conjugal relations enjoying benefits or not of conjugality. I advise keep your mouth in order or you may or may not have repercushins from any direction in any possible weather.
> Every Good Wish, JF

A courier? In Utica? Somebody knocks on his door, some scam artist, carrying an envelope and wearing a badge saying Albany Courier Services, who's instructed brutally by Rocky to put the envelope in the mailbox, with your blouse open down to here. The Professor wants to invite her in for coffee and cookies, and he does, in his mind. And in his mind she comes in and they make sudden hot love, unable to get to the bedroom right there deep inside her in his mind on the shiny linoleum of the kitchen floor.

Russell Martello actually invites her in. She says, I can't, big fella, but I know where you live. Because with your name, Mr. Martello, how can I not return?

This courier, no scam artist is she, had been raised by her immigrant Italian grandmother, who taught her basic Italian vocabulary, mostly the nice words, plus words which refer to what men exclusively think about, my child – men who like women or even their own sex – young or old they think constantly about *il Martello* – the hammer, the tool which means another tool – suspended heavily, men always say, very heavily between their thighs. And *pesce*, the fish. And *piscitello*, the little fish. And la *salsiccia*, the sausage, feminine noun, my child! hot and sweet at the same time. How you say these words to them in the act of love will make them *tanto duro* (very hard) or *come lo spaghetti bagnato* (like a single strand of wet spaghetti.) Beware of the rapist, if you say one of these words to him and make him a limp worm when you tell him his thick sausage is a woman. Because then he chokes you to death. For survival call him *mi grand' amor'*.

*

None of the six, including Russell Martello, who stand at 8:55 pm outside the locked door of Café Romano have seen The Falcon since Giulio Romano's Wake, three weeks before, but they all remember The Falcon's last words at the Wake – a cliché that took on chilling resonance when The Falcon said, "Eat like there's no fuckin' tomorrow." As if they were prisoners about to be executed and were given their last meal – not by their own choice of food, as it happens on Death Row the night before, but prepared and imposed by The Falcon himself: an obscure Sicilian delight known in and around Palermo, *Sfincione di San Vito* – which The Professor was commanded by The Falcon to research and describe for Giulio Romano's mourners.

The Don had prepared it, didn't he? The Don had *cooked* it, didn't he? The fuckin' Don knew damn well how to describe *Sfincione di San Vito*. Sooner or later he will pay. Probably later, too much later, when we're all dead and won't have the satisfaction of dancing in celebration, naked, at high noon on Bleecker Street.

*

How quickly the joke emerges! as Richie unlocks the door. The Falcon gets us here in a group and Russell's here to commit the Columbus Day Massacre, after which Russell eats his gun and puts his brains all over Richie's white wall.

Two days prior, The Professor had undergone three hours of general anesthesia for a problematic double hernia.

The Professor puts his arm around Martello's shoulder.

The Professor says, "It was like saying goodbye to a statue and I walked out back to the hotel in the rain."

Rocky says, "Prof, you're swaying a little. Feeling a little shaky on your feet?"

The Professor says, "Size five narrow in a woman's shoe. Hast thou fingered a woman's shoe? To be or not to be, Rocco babe. Am I right? He lays his head on the cool glass of the table top and says, I am a man of no fortune, and with a name to come."

The Professor closes his eyes and says, "War is the destruction of restaurants, true or false?"

Rose says, "Richie, do you have a blanket? He's shivering."

Richie says, "No blankets, godmother. I'll get a few aprons and something soft for under his head."

The Professor says, "Connie, can you hear me?"

"Yes, dear, I can."

The Professor says, "I love that you call me dear."

Connie says, "We all love you, Prof."

The Professor mumbles something.

Martello says, "What'd he say?"

The Professor lifts his head and says, "If love be not in the house there is nothing." (Puts his head back down as Richie wraps three aprons around The Professor's body and Connie slides a soft towel beneath his head.)

The Professor says, "I am afraid of the rain. I see myself dead in the rain."

Rosie says, "We need to get him in the insane ward at Saint Elizabeth."

The Professor says, "Catherine is dead."

They pull up chairs next to The Prof. Connie and Russell place a reassuring hand on The Prof. Connie on his neck, with a small massage. Russell on his forearm, gently stroking.

Connie says, "I know what this is. I saw this in my uncle after his five hour open heart procedure. He's not nuts."

Russell says, "How come he's talking nuts?"

Rocky says, "He's not nuts, he's just a professor."

The Professor says, "The truth is in kindness."

Richie says, "Who here could possibly disagree with that? How about you, Russell? Are you kind?"

Russell says, "Don't ask, don't tell."

The Professor says, "To … be … men … not … destroyers … only the names of places have dignity."

Russell says, "Yeah. Destroy dignity."

Connie says, "Like my uncle, he's suffering delirium. From the anesthesia – it's a side effect sometimes. He's not gone insane."

The Professor at top volume, "Where is the asshole who thinks he's God? Who wrote that semi-literate garbage the courier brought? I am Burt Lancaster. I will kick his ass from here to eternity. I will make him bleed from all his holes. All ten. Hey, kids! Can you name 'em?"

Rocky says, "I count to eight, unless the eyes count as holes. I'll name my eight, not including the eyes."

Rose says, "Rock, don't name your holes."

Connie asks Richie to dim the recessed overhead lighting to almost nothing. That's step one to counter the delirium. He just needs a little reassurance.

Rose says, "Does he hear us?"

Connie says, "The words go into his ears, but when they enter the mind something happens."

The Professor says, "To be saved by squirrels and blue jays."

Richie says, "I think he's sleeping. Who wants cappuccino and cannoli?"

The Professor raises his head violently and says, "When one's friends hate each other how can there be peace in the world?" Drops his head back down hard. The slow rhythmical breathing of deep sleep. Silence at the Café. No one wants cappuccino and cannoli.

*

Rose to Martello: "Do you respect your substitute godmother?"

"Yes, Godmother."

"Where is your boss?"

"I don't know."

"Why are you here?"

"Because I got the same note you people did."

"You claim to know nothing, Rosario?"

(No response.)

"Rosario, answer me."

"Teresa is not around anymore."

"His wife?"

"Better known as The Mall Fucker."

"Where did she go?"

"The Don said Florida, the ugliest state in the union, he said.

"So I say to him, Why is it ugly?

"Because, he says, it's flatter than a pancake. People go there to become flat, he says.

"To get flat stomachs?

"No, he says, to become flat on the flat ground. They all go there, he said, to Florida, to die."

"Did he tell you this when he sent her down to Florida?"

"No."

"When did you last see The Mall – Teresa?"

"When I drove her to the airport in Syracuse."

"Just you and Teresa?"

"Plus a friend of The Don from the Bronx. Who was flying down there with her for safe keeping. To protect her."

"This friend's name, Rosario? From the Bronx?"

"Jimmy Furio."

"What do you know about him?"

"His nickname."

"Spit it out, Rosario."

"Mazzacristo."

"Do you know what that means, Rosario?"

"No."

"It means Christ killer. Which is how some Italians refer to Jews. Was he a Jew?"

"Not possible."

"Why not?"

"Those types are not allowed in Our Thing. Along with all non-Italians. Not allowed."

"Everyone in your corporation – all like you, Rosario?"

"Whataya mean, like me?"

"All devout Christians in your thing? They go to Mass every Sunday? They go to confession and communion? They renounce Satan and all his works?"

"I won't go to that extreme."

"Did you talk with Mr. Furio on the way to Syracuse?"

"Not really."

"In other words, you had a little conversation?"

"I tried. I said. 'How are you, Jimmy?'"

"And?"

"He said, 'No comment.' I dropped them at the curb of Departures."

"You see them go in?"

"I was minding my own business. *Cazz' mi'*."

Rose says, "Do you renounce Satan and all his works and friends? Answer me."

Richie says, "Godmother, what's really on your mind?"

Connie says, "Why are we here? What does The Don have on his mind?"

Rocky says, "Like The Shadow, my wife knows."

The Professor lifts his head and says, "Two pounds flour. For the dough."

Rocky says, "Don't tell me he's not nuts."

The Professor says, "After people die you have to bury them but you do not have to write about it."

Rocky says, "See what I mean?"

The Professor says, "It's possible to escape from my own wickedness, but impossible to escape from yours. Two cups of warm water." (He sleeps.)

Richie says, "This Jimmy Furio, Russell, he's not a Jew but he kills Jews?"

"Not Jews in general. Just the big Jew who tried to eat part of The Falcon's pie. I am personally not a Jew or a Jew killer."

The Professor: "Dry yeast, not too much. Olive oil, two tablespoons. Two. Don't go overboard."

Rocky: "This is getting pathetic."

Rose: "He's doing the recipe of that thing Don Joseph made, *Sfincione di San Vito*. Write it down, Rock. Rosario, does he have a substitute wife? Somebody move in where Teresa used to live? Where in Florida did she go under the protection of the Christ Killer?"

"I don't know."

Rose: "When was the last time you saw The Falcon?"

"The day before I got the note to come here."

"What was he like?"

"Happy. Extremely. He was wearing cologne, which he never did."

Connie: "Why do you think he wrote to us?"

"Who knows? My personal opinion?"

"No. Your impersonal opinion."

"What?"

"Never mind. Give us your very personal opinion."

"The man loves to play jokes, pranks, whatever you want to call it. It took me weeks to understand the stink in my car. He put rotten eggs and bad gorgonzola under the floorboard of the back seat. Okay? That's how The Falcon rolls in jovial times, God bless him."

Rocky says, "He writes the notes to make us paranoid? This is a joke to massacre us in the Café on Columbus Day? And we all come here like Little Bo Peep and her shitty sheep?"

"Anything is possible with The Falcon except pedophilia, if that's your reference to Little Bo Peep."

Rose: "Did you see her at the house?"

"Who?"

"Don't play dumb. The Italian visitor."

The Professor says, "For the condiments: One pound of sausage, sans casings. If I find out you're lying to me, Joey, I'm gonna kill somebody."

Rosario: "I feel she's on the second floor where the Floridian wife used to be."

Rose: "Your feeling based on?"

"I had to go to the drugstore to pick up a prescription. I peek in the bag they put it in: Viagra."

Richie brings cappuccino and cannolis for everyone, "whether you want it or not, my friends. Shall we get down to facts while we're all together? My grandfather died at Hospice. Like all Hospice deaths in Utica, it was looked into. He died after I visited him. She, the Italian, went in to 'see my great uncle,' she told the nurses. One of them takes her down the hall to his room because it was time to check on his vitals. He had no vitals. He was already dead. Proves the Italian is innocent. She's alive. She and the Don are an item. They're doing the job. She's there on the second floor at Taylor Ave, where the wife used to be. No detective story here, folks. Nothing dark and bloody here."

The Professor, eyes closed: "Pitted black olives. Diced. Half pound. I always feel trapped biologically."

Rose: "Write it down, Rock."

The Professor: "One cup white wine. Nothing left here but women. I prefer it with sausage. Not potatoes. I do not love God with three medium onions sliced. The air is full of women."

Rocky: "The part about God he does not love with onions? That part of the recipe?"

Connie: "What your grandfather did, Rich, after he came over. That was dark and bloody."

"We all know the story, Connie. Let's not beat a dead horse."

"Big deal, Connie. He has a wife plus a kid over there. He comes here and starts all over again. From scratch. To tell the truth, from snatch."

"America the beautiful.

"Land of opportunity.

"Sweet land of liberty.

"Of thee Giulio sang."

"He's here with a new and better erection."

"The Old World is a crime against better erections."

"Over there, only death frees you from a marriage made in Hell."

"Giulio's marriage over there was not necessarily choking him to death."

"Granted, the odds in any marriage, let's say his first marriage was slowly choking him to death."

"Screw the wife and child in Italy, I sympathize."

"Immigration with her legs wide saying give it to me, big boy, which was the problem back then and today."

"The Mexicans pouring in."

"The Ragheads pouring in."

"The Spics."

"I say people should stay in their diseased native soil."

"The Old Country is a bad wife."

"He's dead. Giulio is dead. We're beating off a dead horse."

"Beating off?"

"You approve he dumped the wife and kid over there?"

"Speaking of horses. Let's get off our high horse. Three out of four man and woman marriages go down the toilet. No problem. Get divorced as many times as you need to. Now the gay people of America want to get married?"

"Proves they're nuts."

"Nuts like a fruit cake."

"Fruit cake is a slur against people like my cousin, who's a great guy. Don't slur my fucked up cousin."

"Tony's gay? Tony never got married doesn't prove he's gay. Just because he's drop dead handsome doesn't prove he's gay, although those people tend to have all the looks. Bastards."

"Tony might be gay, but at least he's not an immigrant come over to suck out our … every drop swallowed. Our blood. Our jobs."

"Let's not get into hypocrisy concerning oral-you-know-what. Let's not be hypocrites."

"The subject here is immigration. Forget about oral sex, if that's possible."

"Which it is not. I should know."

"Speaking personally, Russell?"

"No comment."

"Which means he speaks personally. My condolences, Rosario."

"We are a nation of immigrants and oral sex fiends. This is the meaning of American history."

"My father immigrated for oral sex?"

"Too many Mexicans pouring in."

"The fuckin' Blacks were not immigrants."

"Likewise the fuckin' Redskins, so-called Native Americans."

"Why the f-word, Rosario? What did the Black people ever do to you, Rosario? Put a gun to your head? Let's not get into the hypocrisy of who puts a gun to whose head."

"I'm sorry, Godmother."

"You carrying right now, Russell?"

"No comment."

"O that this too too solid flesh would melt …"

The Prof is awake with his gibberish.

"He's quoting Shakespeare."

"Like I said. Gibberish."

"Or that the Everlasting had not fix'd his canon against self-slaughter."

"The Everlasting is the Big Man upstairs, am I right?"

"You're not wrong, Rocky."

"Self-slaughter is what normal people call suicide. Am I right, Richie?"

"You got it, Rocky."

"I like self-slaughter, Rich. I love it. Suicide if you never heard the word gives you no picture. Self-slaughter – who could not get that right off the bat?"

The Prof is unhappy dreaming of self-murder.

"In this shithole world, Russell, who isn't unhappy?"

"The language, boys."

"The Prof is cracked."

"Nah. Just talking poetry."

"Time to take him to the bug house."

"Dear friends, let's get back on track."

"The oral sex track?"

"The *Sfincione di San Vito* track?"

"The Falcon disappeared his wife track?"

"The Falcon's affair with the Italian beauty track?"

"The Falcon's reason for bringing us here track?"

"The immigration track?"

"The gay track?"

"The Spics are overwhelming us track?"

The Professor: "She's very late. Where is she? I drown in my anxiety."

"I thought he was single."

"He is."

"He lives alone?"

"Always has."

The Prof: "You do not have to write about an undertaker nor the business of burial in a foreign country."

"Who died?"

"His mind."

"What foreign country?"

"His mind."

"We had conversation this morning. Who's against that?"

"Conversation about what *exactly*?"

"Who knows? Who cares? The conversation, it's a pleasure by itself. Ping Pong back and forth. Conversation is a pleasure always unless there is hatred in the air. Which there wasn't hatred here in Richie's domain. We talk. We zig. We zag. Am I right, Russell?"

"Love is in the air," Russell says. "Do one of you, at least one of you, love me?"

The Professor says, "Paradise is *spezzato* … it exists in fragments… unexpected excellent sausage … the smell of mint … Ladro the night cat … this hour at Café Romano …"

"The Falcon pranked us, but we overcame, as Martin Luther King mentioned. We won. The Falcon is not God. He lost, and we had fun."

Rose says, "At my age, all my friends are dying, left and right. This morning, with you, I am not dying."

"Amen to that."

The Professor: "*Il vento nostro fratello, la pioggia nostra sorella …*"

"Godmother, what did he say?"

"The wind is our brother. The rain is our sister."

The Professor: "*Il bello è difficile.*"

"What?"

"Beauty is … he said."

"What, godmother? Beauty is what?"

"Beauty, he said, is difficult."

6.

Decades Later

RICHIE IN HIS pajamas stands at the kitchen window, 6:30 A.M., looking out at the feeder. He says, "They left me."

Connie says, "Who left you?"

He says, "The Rubythroated – they're gone. Hail to thee, blithe Spirit! Bird thou never wert …"

"A poet again?"

"Yeah."

"Your humming birds will be back next spring."

"I won't."

"You won't what?"

"Be back next spring."

"Dying again, Rich?"

"I'm half in love with easeful death."

"Another poet?"

"You seriously think, Connie, I could pull words like that out of my own head?"

"You'll live to a hundred, Rich, like it or not. Oatmeal or eggs?"

"No."

"Which one no? The oatmeal or the eggs?"

"Both no."

"Your prostate act up again last night?"

"Eleven times I peed since midnight."

"You counted?"

"Since the pandemic I can't stand American breakfast food."

"What's the pandemic have to do with it?"

"A lot."

"You're scaring me, Richie."

He opens the refrigerator. Stares in for awhile. Removes a container of last night's Pasta Bolognese. Many little chunks of blazing hot Italian sausage. He says, "Descending to my Dago roots, Connie."

"At 6:30 in the morning? Your roots?"

He spoons the pasta into a bowl. Inserts it into the Microwave. Sets timer for one minute, but does not press START. He says, "What are the Eskimos eating for breakfast in northern Greenland? Raw seal meat, Connie."

"This is my husband."

"On the other hand." Removes the bowl from the oven before he's pushed START. Takes the bowl to the table as Connie digs into her yogurt, granola and strawberries.

"At least heat it up, Rich."

"That cold thing you eat every morning. Does it even have a name?"

"What's wrong? In addition to your departed birds, who look like overgrown Bumble Bees?"

"She makes a crack about The Rubythroated. Jealous? Afraid they'll replace you in my heart?" Takes the bowl back to the Microwave. Presses START. "You win, Connie. You win."

"You die, Richie? In April you return – on Easter Sunday like the Risen Christ."

"She goes to High Mass every Sunday. And she talks like that."

"Long after I return to the Father, Rich, you'll – I have something on my mind. Let's sell the Café and get rid of – I don't even want to say his name. Get him off our back once and for all. We move to Vero Beach, where all your cousins, who love you despite your hatred of Trump."

"The cousins are a good thing, despite they get on their knees for Trump. The Rubythroated – those little miracles – I've seen them make right angle turns at top speed without loss of speed. Can you imagine a football running back who –"

"Can't stomach that sport."

"Nonstop across the Gulf of Mexico because what choice do they have? To Southern Mexico. Central America."

"They don't winter with the Florida Fascists?"

"Don't mock The Rubythroated, Constance. I'm gonna eat this."

"Have you called your shrink? Call Chris. You used to come back from Chris lighter. Call. Tell him you're dying again. He helped you numerous times in the past when you started dying on the exact day before you had an appointment with him."

"I never told Chris the total truth."

"Which you didn't reveal to Chris about our association with –"

"Don't say his name. I don't want to hear it."

"JF. Joe Furillo. Don Joseph (The Falcon) Furillo."

"Stop. I'm eating."

"You sure are, Rich."

"Italian food improves in the leftover state."

"Like you, Rich."

"Don't flatter me with my mouth full."

"How about me in the leftover state? I'm not the woman I used to be."

"You still look terrific."

"Still? I'm old."

"Don't say his name or his nickname because I don't want to hear it again, especially when I'm thinking about what I have to do today on behalf of his birthday. He says to me, 'Surprise me, Richie.' I'm gonna surprise him, Connie."

"He did a lot on our behalf."

"My shrink. Yeah."

"No. I'm referring to the one who shall not be named."

"What balls! Including the females. Who also have big ones. Across the Gulf their wings beating 53 times a second nonstop over fatal water. You're making me talk with my mouth full."

"You just made that up? 53 times a second?"

"People at Cornell who study birds."

"Bird scientists?"

"Don't even think his name."

"You could've been one of those bird scientists, if you went to college. Because what don't you know about birds?"

"I never wanted college. My high school fantasy was to become a pastry chef. Which I did with his assistance, who got us the Café when the landlord tried to gouge us on the price of the building. You know this. He made the landlord an offer he couldn't refuse, as they say in the movies. Which you could guess what it was. I'll never spell it out because you don't need that burden. The only thing I loved in high school was you, who took awhile to give me the time of day, but when you did … plus I loved my poetry class. The Romantics, yeah. Pastries, poetry, and you.

Who needed college? I'm almost totally happy now at this stage of my life except for that psychopath. A thousand years of that guy in our heads."

"Plus your birds. These days, above all, your birds."

"The female Ruby is bigger than the male. You don't know this. You don't observe with the binoculars. You don't read the books. She has a longer beak. He gets the ruby throat – he gets beauty in compensation. Which is the way it usually is in the bird world, but not in our marriage. Plus, the female Ruby is larger in body dimensions than her spouse. Same thing in our –"

"Don't go there. Don't start, Richard."

"My wild Irish Rose can't take a joke. For your information bird science is ornithology. Ornithologists practice ornithology."

"The words just roll off his tongue. His flexible tongue."

"Where there's a tongue there's a way. Tomorrow for breakfast a salami sandwich. I have to finish this. Don't talk."

"Don't wolf it. You're wolfing."

"The Rubythroated consoles you, Con, next spring, once I'm gone."

"Want your coffee?"

"All packed for tonight? Can't wait to see our son."

"Packed last week. He did a lot for us, Rich."

"Andrew did a lot just by being our son."

"I meant, you know … not Andrew but the psychopath."

"Which is why I'm planning special in honor of his 75th."

"The Falcon."

"Don't."

"JF did a lot for us."

"Don't even say the initials, Connie."

"Thanks to him, whose initials are forbidden, we paid no real estate taxes for years on the Café or our house. I don't have to remind you."

"So why remind me? He saved us in the six figures."

"Then we saved him."

"He collected. Oh, yeah."

"He has always insisted on paying for the endless pastries and cakes, which we never would've charged him for. The birthdays, the weddings, the funerals, the first communions. The quiet parties with so-called family up from New York. We know who they are."

"Because, Con, he was biding his time for major debt collection. Which let's not talk about it. We never talked about it ever since it happened. What's the point of talking? We developed selective dementia."

"Russell is the truth you held back from Chris."

"On behalf of the psychopath and Russell, also a psycho, I violated the ninth commandment: Thou shalt not bear false witness."

"Will Russell be at the birthday party?"

"Is the Secret Service always there to protect the president? Our debt will never be paid in full. For people like The Falcon, you owe a favor? The principal is infinite. There will be major collections worse than the Russell thing. Eventually he'll make me do murder to close our account."

"Let's cut the baloney about the Secret Service, Rich, and say the words for once. Russell did how many murders over the years? Thirty, it is said. Three years ago when the one whose name can't be said – he stopped biding his time. He collected to save Russell, who was observed by an innocent bystander –"

"Stop, Connie."

"Executing Garramondo –"

"Stop, Connie."

"You testify Russell at the time of the hit was at the Café eating his three cannoli. I was in the court room. Everyone at court laughs, Rich, when on the stand you mention three cannoli, including Russell laughs, but the Garramondo family does not laugh."

"Connie, want to cut the baloney, once and for all? According to old school Catholics, like us, we had a choice. Three years ago concerning Russell we rationalized murder. We succumbed. No more of this. I have work to do. Something with my hands instead of wallowing in this fucking guilt."

"In all our years, Rich, never have I heard you say the f-word. Sorry I brought it up. What's the point? We can't change the past. Can I help you make the cake? I could come to the Café and at least keep you company."

"Stay home, get the house in order before we leave. Please pack for me. I need to make this cake in isolation."

"What kind of cake are you baking?"

"In the style of my grandmother."

"The triple-layered rum cake?"

He pauses.

He says, "With a variation to express my individual genius."

"These people, Rich, with their g-d nicknames? They do you a favor, which you definitely asked for, let's be honest. Then somebody has to do a bigger favor back, or somebody ends up in the trunk of a lousy used car."

"Me in the trunk, Connie."

"We got ours, once. Forty years ago. He gets his forever."

"Until death gives us all a break."

*

They leave Utica for Albany, where they'll fly to Boston, change there for Toronto and change again for St. John's Newfoundland, where expatriate son Andrew will drive them far through the night to Carbonear, his home and site of his book store, The Green Door – featuring books, in his Canada-famous advertisement, "that will tempt even those who desire a book in the hand as much as two bullets in the back of the head."

"Leave" Utica would have been Connie's word, who is in the dark. "Flee" Utica would have been Richie's word, who knows what Connie does not yet know. Say it always this way: Utica, New York – one of 12 Uticas in the United States, distinguished from all others by *Time* magazine as the "City that God forgot."

Nearing Albany – Richie at the wheel, Connie dozing. She awakes. She says, "So how really did it go at his party, aside from repeating five times, 'fine, Connie.'"

"Fine, Connie."

"Everyone enjoyed the cake?"

"Voraciously."

"Were there guests aside from The Altar Boy?"

"One other. From New York."

"The Angel of Disembowelment?"

"No."

"The Sausage Grinder?"

"No."

"Don't tell me –"

"I'm telling you."

"The Boss of all Bosses came to Utica?"

"*Capo di tutti capi*."

"The Prime Mover himself?"

"Himself."

"All three praised your art?"

"Eventually The Falcon ate –"

"So now we can say The Falcon?"

"Eventually The Prime Mover ate two pieces, but The Altar Boy tried to resist. He tells me of his condition. He says, 'My sugar, Richie. My doctor, he's almost happy. These doctors, they have cold hearts. He says to me, Mr. Martello, you got diabetes. It hurts me to know I can't eat your beautiful cake. I got no choice.' So I say to Russell, I commiserate, because I have a sugar problem myself through the roof."

"Since when do you have a sugar problem, Rich? You wanted him for some reason to feel bonded with you?"

"No."

"Why lie?"

As he pulls into long term parking at Albany International, Richie says, "When we get to the boarding area I'll tell you."

She says, "I don't like the sound of that."

He says, "Was there a lot of garlic in the Bolognese? I have a strong garlic taste."

"Some," she says, "but you ate that, what? Ten hours ago? It's not that. Don't blame my cooking."

At their gate he rushes to the Men's Room, almost not making it. When he returns she says, "Now tell me why you lied to Russell."

Richie says, "There are humming birds in Newfoundland."

"Don't change the subject. Why lie to Russell?"

"I didn't want to eat the cake."

"I sympathize, Rich, who enjoys their own cooking?"

"You could say that."

"What are you holding back, Richard?"

He pauses. He opens his phone. Closes it. Says, "What are we doing for New Year's Eve?"

She says, "Rich, this is the middle of July."

He opens his phone again: "Look at this." A picture of Russell about to fork a large piece of cake into his enormous mouth.

Richie says, "Russell goes, 'Good Lord, over three years no dessert. Not even a little cookie because I don't want to go to the other side because of my sugar.' So then, Connie, he holds up the forkful and says, 'How could one piece hurt me? Or two if I don't do it again for another three years? God willing I'm still here in three years.'

"Meanwhile, Connie, The Prime Mover and The Falcon watch Russell go to town, but they don't eat. Russell says between mouthfuls, 'I'm in another reality. Go ahead, Richie, how much can it hurt you? As the Jews always say, This is to die for. I hate those words.'

"Then The Prime Mover says to The Falcon, 'This baker friend of yours is a front for a Jew-owner behind the bakery? What is it in this country that the Jews are not behind? They're competing with Our Thing.'

"The Falcon says, 'Stefano, Stefano, this baker is also the owner, and he's not a Jew.'

"The Prime Mover says, 'He's claiming diabetes, which I'm thinking maybe, maybe not. You trust this guy, Joe?'

"The Falcon replies, 'For years I trust this guy who is not a Jew, by any stretch of the imagination.'"

Richie sweats. He's cold. He says, "Can I have a sip of your water?"

She says, "You drank almost 32 ounces on the way down."

He drinks. He says, "I don't feel so good. I think I'm going to –" Walks rapidly to the Men's Room where he vomits violently.

When he returns, he says, "Something I ate didn't agree –" Jogs to the Men's Room and vomits dryly.

When he returns she says, "You don't look right."

He sits back and closes his eyes. She takes his hand. He opens his phone again. "Then The Prime Mover says to the Falcon, 'Like Reagan said, Joe, trust but verify.' He comes over to me and puts a revolver to my head. The ... The Prime Mover says, 'You understand my verification? Eat the cake.' After I eat, The Falcon and The Prime Mover eat. Big pieces. Slabs. Me a sliver."

"How could it be the cake?" she says. "By the way, Rich, was everyone wearing masks?"

"Those people, Connie, are not democrats."

He shows her another picture, taken by Russell, of Richie eating.

From Toronto to St. John's he suffers two bouts of diarrhea. In the tight space of the airplane toilet, with someone knocking furiously at the door, as he shivers, thinking in his rising stench, Just a sliver. This is worse than my brains on The Falcon's table. At the airport in St. John's, diarrhea again.

On the way to Carbonear he says, "I understand that in Newfoundland there are nine Moose per square inch. Andrew, do you know the street to Iceland? Let's take it to Iceland. Be careful of the tricky turn off to the Gulf of Mexico."

Connie from the back seat leans and puts her hand on Richie's shoulder. She says, "Richie, I pray you're just joking."

Richie says, "Joking about what?! I will not quarantine in Andrew's palatial quarters for 52 days. I will do my time, thank you very much, at The Green Door, where I will read all the books. After which, you heard it from me, we will drive for nine and a half hours north to the Gulf of St. Lawrence, to St. Barbe. There, we will take a ferry – that is not homophobia, don't tell me it is, kids – to where, Andrew, my man?"

"To Labrador, Dad. To Blanc Sablon."

"This kid of mine speaks French. Your mother and I, your so-called parents, are not French. Got it, Andy? But we love you nevertheless by free American choice."

Connie says, "Is there a hospital in Carbonear?"

Andrew says, "We're going there directly."

Richie says, "From Labrador, a planet named in honor of our dog who died an hour ago, we fly to Goose Bay. From there to guess what, kids! Boston! Connecting to the Gulf of Mexico, Iceland's fair and balmy capitol."

Andrew forces a laugh: "You're not feeling well, Dad, but you're still a funny dude."

Richie says, "There are no humming birds in Scandinavia, but there's a bird up there according to ancient legend that I wanted to see all my endless life."

"What's that, Dad?"

Richie says, "My sister's birthday is coming up. Do they allow birthdays in Newfoundland?"

Connie in the back seat weeps quietly. Richie doesn't have a sister. She says, "How long to the hospital?"

"Almost there."

"Go faster."

Richie says, "What's the hurry?"

*

Andrew sits in the hospital cafeteria, about to eat lunch as he watches the TV monitor running *CNN Headline News*:

Wolf Blitzer here in The Situation Room.

This just in from our affiliate in Utica, New York: The alleged supreme leader of the Mafia in the United States, boss of all bosses, as he is known, Stefano (The Prime Mover) Migliacci, is dead in Brooklyn. Cause of death, end-stage shock triggered by suspected poisoning. In Utica, his long-time associate, Joe The Falcon Furillo and his notorious enforcer, Russell The Altar Boy Martello, also reported dead. Cause, again, end-stage shock triggered by unconfirmed poisoning. Anonymous gangland sources say that The Prime Mover had journeyed to Utica two days ago to celebrate the birthday of pal Furillo. Utica Police on deep background tell us they seek to question Richard Romano, famed upstate New York pastry chef, whose whereabouts are at this time unknown. An anonymous FBI official, intimate for years with gangland America, had this to say: The suspicious deaths of these brutal men is not a crime to be solved. It is a crime to be celebrated.

Andrew abandons his lunch untouched and rushes toward his father's room where, in the hallway outside his door, he finds Doctor DuBois explaining to his mother that her husband's symptoms track closely with Arsenic poisoning. "A garlic taste signals the onset of such. Psychological symptoms, hallucinations and incoherence, though unusual, are indicative of potentially lethal consequences. Let me be specific. I am concerned about his stage of shock. There are three. Stage one is mild and commonly experienced. It does not require medical intervention. Stage three is irreversible and ends in rapid death. Stage two is your husband's. We're doing all we can to freeze this stage and relieve him altogether from the condition. Fluids for severe dehydration and steeply declining blood pressure. Medications with unpronounceable names administered as we speak."

Connie says, "He's going to recover, you're saying."

"We are hopeful at this time."

The doctor leaves and Andrew informs Connie of what he's heard on CNN and asks if Dad made a birthday cake for these "scum bags." Because Dad is "sought by law enforcement."

Connie says, "He did. He ate some himself. He had no choice. Long story. Oh my God, Andrew."

They go into the room. Connie in grief and anger blurts out, "Richie, you baked a rum cake for those awful people and they died. Now look at you. We wanted to close our account with The Falcon, I confess, but not in this way. Oh my God, Richie."

Richie says, "In the spring, I arise on the third day from the dead in Central America."

Though hooked up intravenously for fluids and medications, he is not connected to a machine that would keep him alive should he plunge into extremity. There is no DNR note (Do Not Resuscitate) attached to his bed.

Richie says, "Andrew, pull the plug."

Andrew says, "Dad, there is no plug."

Connie says, "Give him a few days. He'll be fine."

Silence in the room.

Richie says, "The circumpolar bird of the Arctic ... the Snow Bunting ... feeder on the tundra ... eating the tundra ... ghost bird of my soul ..."

"Where, Dad?"

"Pack me up, Connie. We leave in 30 minutes."

Silence in the room.

Richie says, "Some go to San Francisco, with flowers in their yellow hair. Come along with me and Perry Como."

"Where, Dad?"

"With Eskimos our guide –
With seal meat in our backpacks –
We seek The Snow Bunting –
In the farthest North of Greenland –"

*

The FBI contacts Chief Robinson of the Utica PD to request that he look into, "whenever convenient," the role of Richard Romano in the deaths of three Mafia powers: "No rush, Chief." Robinson immediately contacts Chief of Detectives Joseph Caruso – Romano's friend since childhood – to tell him that his "pal is way up there in Newfoundland with his life hanging by a thread and a charge of triple murder about to drop on his head. You're going up there, Joe, before it's too late to save his good name."

When Caruso arrives he finds that Richie has rallied strongly. Caruso's first words are, "I was worried sick about you. You look almost good."

"So why worry, Joey? What's on your mind?"

"Cake is on my mind."

"When we get back to Utica, I'll make you happy. Is your divorce final?"

"I have a formality we need to get through. A waste of time, but we have to do it for legal reasons. Rich, I never wanted the divorce, I thought I told you that."

"Legal? What legal?"

"I'm turning on this thing for legal reasons. Answer as fast as you can because this is stressing me out."

"You're beginning to scare me, Joe."

"You baked a cake for the big shot of Utica? For his birthday?"

"Yes."

"A triple-decker rum cake?"

"Yes."

"The delicious one your maternal grandmother used to make?"

"Yes."

"The one she used to make for my birthday, without fail?"

"Yes."

"This cake you made was eaten by The Falcon and the biggest of all big shots, known as The Prime Mover, plus our high school sorta friend, the religious fanatic with a lot of blood on his hands?"

"Yes."

"Plus you ate it too?"

"Yes."

"You made this cake exactly the way your grandmother made this cake?"

"Yes."

"No extra ingredient?"

"None."

"Those three died after eating your cake. You know this."

"Yes."

"A day after the death party you and Connie come up here, the end of the world, where you get sicker than a dog. But as you sit here before me –"

"I am alive."

"Anybody force you to eat the cake?"

"No."

"You – Rich, if you inserted poison in the cake, you wouldn't eat the cake with your free will if you yourself inserted poison and you knew you yourself inserted the poison. Am I right or am I wrong?"

"Totally right."

"Rich, someone put the poison in, but it wasn't you, Richie."

"It wasn't me, Joey."

"Forgive me. It's a chain of command type question I have to ask. Was Connie ever alone with the cake – out of your view of the cake?"

"No."

"Thank God. We're dealing with a mystery. Your so-called involvement with the demise of – you had no involvement in the sad deaths of those rotten bastards. Which is my conclusion to this formality."

"When we get back to Utica, Joey C, come over for dinner."

"I will! But tell the fantastic Connie no special ingredient." (They grin.)

"Two love birds, Rich, shacking up from the beginning and still are."

"We're married."

"Married or not, you two shacked up at the beginning and still are and I say, God bless those who shack up and stay shacked up for life. You agree?"

"Did you shut the recorder off?"

"I forgot to."

"Good."

*

On the way home from Newfoundland, Connie suggests a vacation to Oneida Lake, where Giulio Romano had owned, free and clear, a large two-story house on Sylvan Beach, which he had willed exclusively to Connie. He told the lawyer to write that she needed a home of her own to escape from Richie when he became "too much." The lawyer urged Giulio to specify, for legal purposes, the conditions and causes of "too much," and Giulio said, "They know." And indeed they knew, without fail, when Richie became "too much," and for forty years, two weekends per month, they escaped to Sylvan Beach.

"Too much" describes several behaviors – most notably Richie's desire for sex at all hours of the day, his insistence that he cook dinner three times per week, the same dish – spaghetti aglia e olio and fried shallots, with sausages and meatballs on the side, and his refusal to take the wheel, whenever they drove to Sylvan Beach, so that he could gaze at the passing landscape without endangering their safety. To gaze in silence except to exclaim, "There's another one! The woodchucks are taking over this state. Better them than people."

Mostly, "too much" was defined comically as "now *that's* too much," referring to nothing at all, "so let's go to Sylvan Beach," where they spent their evenings at the Midway, to eat hot dogs and cotton candy and take carnival rides. He, the bumper boats, the bumper cars, and kiddieland. She, alone, on the Ferris Wheel, tallest on the East Coast, and the Rollercoaster, scariest on the East Coast. She had given him a St. Anthony medal, but it did not ease his fear of dying and he would not accompany her on her rides. He'd prefer, he said, and St. Anthony agreed, to play Mini-Golf.

On the way home from Newfoundland, Too Much Romano appears painfully when he says, "Venice, Connie, Venice, before we were married. The gondolas cost too much that year, but we took them anyway, and frequently. The gondolas were like us. Romantic. We made it through our nine days by not eating lunch. Remember?"

"How could I forget?"

"Coffee and a pastry at mid-day, except once – except once when your favorite gondolier invited us to lunch. Remember? Remember Aldo?"

She says, "Who?"

"You don't remember Aldo?"

"No."

She changes the subject abruptly to The Professor's mysterious message. Four words emailed to Connie in Newfoundland: "Mind the closing door." It wasn't until they'd gotten home to Utica that they'd understood it was The Professor's way of saying goodbye. His last words before he took his own life.

At Sylvan Beach, she said, "That St. Anthony medal I gave you? It belongs around your neck." And he replied, "You believe that stuff – sorry to call it 'stuff.' That hocus-pocus. This St. Anthony you told me is the saint of lost objects. He will help me to find something I lost? What have I lost?" She said, "In Venice, Rich. You lost your soul. Since we left Newfoundland you've lost it again, thinking about Venice. About something that never happened in Venice. We had great dinners in Venice. We had great strolls in Venice. We had great sex in Venice. That's what I remember about Venice."

"Who were you thinking about, Connie, when we went at it in Venice?"

"I wasn't thinking," she said, "just feeling your hands and mouth all over me. Not to mention your – just us, we became our bodies without minds."

He said, "Really, Connie? Really?"

The long trip home to Utica and the subsequent long weekend at Sylvan Beach were dominated by Richie's gloom. The Professor's suicide, which Richie attributed to incurable loneliness. "He needed romance, but never got it. (Unlike us, Rich.) The door was always closing, Connie, and he did 'mind' it, but what good did that do? And the passing, the sweetest people I've ever known." And Connie said, "They were the sweetest, Rose and Rocky. First Rocky and then one week later Rose, who seemed so healthy."

Rich says, "I still can't get over their deaths. I miss them. I'll miss them until I go."

"At least, Rich, Rocky doesn't have to suffer the ups and downs of his beloved Yankees."

"Nice try, Connie, but I'm not amused. I wasn't amused by Aldo either. Still am not amused by Aldo. Maybe if I had been good at learning Italian, like you. You got fluent in two months of study, night and day, before we went to Venice. If I had studied like you maybe I would have understood what you and Aldo were talking about on the gondola and at lunch, where I was out to lunch."

She says, "What does this mythical Aldo have to do with the deaths of The Prof and your godparents?"

"I'll tell you what. In Venice, your interaction with your favorite gondolier, with Aldo –"

"Who's Aldo?"

"That's when I started to die. Aldo started off by calling me Signor Romano. Then he started to call me Tenente, the Lieutenant you said that meant. Was he your general?"

"Christ, Rich. Forty-two years later you're stewing over someone you call Aldo? Who you think I had something –"

"I stayed at the pensione to take an afternoon nap, still jet-lagged. You, remember? You went out to so-called shop. You come back with nothing. How come?"

"Christ, Rich. What are you talking about?"

"I wasn't the one who went shopping in Venice for three hours and bought nothing. Did you spend three hours with Aldo?"

"Anything I wanted was too expensive."

"But Aldo – he didn't cost a penny."

"A thousand years later you're losing it about what I don't know what you're talking about. Some gondolier who I can't recall even what he looked like, who took us to lunch? I did not betray you in Italy with someone you call Aldo."

"Or anyone else? Anyone in this country?"

"I love only you. Always did."

"I ask if you betrayed me with anyone in this country and you say you never stopped loving me. Which doesn't answer my question."

"Rich."

"It's eating me up, Connie. The jealousy. Only death –"

"We're not dead yet."

"I still like to watch you move."

"Really, Rich? I like to watch you move too. Especially from behind."

"Really? You never told me that. How come?"

"I *have* told you that. Arturo. Your madness triggers my memory. Arturo. Not Aldo. Arturo was the gondolier who took us to lunch. He called *you* the General. He said *he* was only a lieutenant. He said we were crazy for each other. Arturo, a man in his 60s, at least. Venice's oldest gondolier, he said."

*

On the beach. Night. Wrapped in blankets. Cold wind off the lake.

"We got off, thanks to Joey Caruso and the FBI, which never gave a damn. We did the country a favor."

"We?"

"We. You were an accessory after the fact. You knew and didn't turn me in."

"As if I would."

"The law doesn't care about your loyalty. You're a criminal too."

"Cotton candy still on my face, Richie."

"I have a method for that. Like in the old days when we were young."

"You murdered three men."

"I murdered three murderers. Russell, though, I feel sorry for Russell."

"We have to live with that, Rich, especially you. They should give you a medal. Russell, though."

"They would have killed me at the drop of a hat. Russell. He gave *you* the proof of the Italian visitor. Why *you*, Connie, privately? Not *me*? The picture Russell took of her at the security gate. At JFK. Holding up a card with the date. Then a picture of her at the other side of the security gate. She was safe. Going home to Naples. Safe and sound. Why you, not me? I never understood why you and no one else, with the exception, no doubt, of The Falcon."

"I have no idea. He was always sweet on me. Are we going down the paranoia route again? This cotton candy requires the old method. Sooner rather than later."

"It's too cold out here. Let's go in and rehearse the old method, like the old days. I'm having ideas for the cotton candy and beyond. We should put cotton candy on – especially on –"

"Let's make believe, Rich, that there are people walking by and under the blankets we're doing something and you say, pretty loud, Is it in? And I say, loud, Deeper, Rich. Deeper."

"Connie, we never do the things we want to do. We never do such things."

"Rich."

"What?"

"What is imagination for?"

"Connie, what is the truth for? Raw and unfiltered?"

"Tell me, Rich, I tremble."

"You mock?"

"With love. Always."

"My sex drive for you? Desperate distraction. My cooking? Distraction. My refusal to take the wheel on the way to Sylvan Beach? Distraction."

"I'm on pins and needles, Rich. Distraction from what?"

"Mockery can't protect you this time."

"Distraction from what?"

"Fear. That you never really liked me."

"Mental abandonment? Why not divorce?"

"Never wanted divorce."

"Why not?"

"Fear."

"Of what?"

"Losing your nearness. As it says in the song (sings): the nearness of you."

"You fear me and need to stay close at the same time? All these years you're ripped up? Kinda nuts?"

"How many years have we been coming here? The odors and the sounds of Sylvan Beach, they haven't changed."

"We have, Rich. For better or for worse?"

"I need to go to the market."

"To cook for distraction?"

"To cook for us."

"What?"

"*Sfincione di San Vito.* Whether you like me or not."

"I love you and I like you."

"People either love or hate. They don't ever 'like.'"

"Rich."

"It'll be terrific!"

"What?"

"*Sfincione di San Vito.*"

"Like us, Rich, terrific."

"Yes. Sort of."

"We're talking too much, Rich. Let's go in and deal with the cotton candy."

"Now?"

"Now."

Acknowledgements

Jody McAuliffe, without whom not.

About the Author

After ground-breaking work as a literary theorist, Frank Lentricchia changed his focus in the early 1990s and since has written a number of novels that explore ethnic and artistic identity within the context of contemporary American political disasters (Vietnam, Iraq) and in *Manhattan Meltdown* the global crisis of Covid-19. His books have been translated into Spanish, Japanese, Korean, Chinese, and Turkish. He was born to working-class parents in Utica, New York, first in the extended family to attend college. He lives in Durham, North Carolina, and was elected to the American Academy of Arts and Sciences in 2013.

FICTION BY FRANK LENTRICCHIA

The Falcons of Desire
Manhattan Meltdown
The Glamour of Evil / A Place in the Dark
The Morelli Thing
The Dog Killer of Utica
The Accidental Pallbearer
The Portable Lentricchia
The Sadness of Antonioni
The Italian Actress
The Book of Ruth
Lucchesi and The Whale
The Music of the Inferno
The Knifemen
Johnny Critelli
The Edge of Night (faux memoir/fiction)

Printed by Imprimerie Gauvin
Gatineau, Québec